# Squirrel & Swan

GS -

M. D. Archer

Published by M. D. Archer © December 2018 All Rights Reserved.

www.mda-author.com

Squirrel & Swan: Devious Things is a work of fiction. Names, places and incidents, except those clearly in the public domain, are products of the author's imagination, or are used fictitiously. Any resemblance to actual persons, names, places or incidents is purely coincidental. No part of this book may be reproduced in any form or by any electronic or mechanical means, including information storage and retrieval systems, without written permission from the author, except for the use of brief quotations in a book review.

# S & S Investigations

#1 Squirrel & Swan Precious Things
#2 Squirrel & Swan Devious Things
#3 Squirrel & Swan Hidden Things

# 1

On the eighth floor of a building in Auckland's central business district, Harry King sat in his cramped cubicle—he was one of the smaller cogs in the corporate machine—and blew out an exasperated gust of air. Leaning back in his chair, he ran his fingers through his greasy hair and considered the ceiling for a moment before returning his gaze to his computer screen.

There it was. No doubt about it.

Harry stared at the spreadsheet in front of him, chewing on the hangnail tormenting his left thumb until his phone jumped to life, throbbing with the drum and bass tune he'd downloaded for his ringtone.

"Shit," he whispered to himself.

One, no two, annoyed faces popped up over their cubicles to glare at Harry.

"Sorry."

Harry sent the call to voicemail then pushed back into a stretch as his stomach let out an angry growl. He dropped his arms to run sweaty hands along the legs of his pants, wondering if he should get something to eat or push through. If he didn't eat he wouldn't be able to concentrate, but home time wasn't too far away. He returned to the spreadsheet. The rows of numbers and formulas gave him satisfaction, like they always did—a buzz; a nerdy thrill. They made sense, neat and ordered and behaving in ways that he could predict.

At least they used to.

Now, right in front of him, was a discrepancy that he couldn't explain. Had his spreadsheet been corrupted somehow? Was there something wrong with his algorithm or had he made some other mistake? It had never happened before, but he'd been overdoing it a bit over the last few weeks. Maybe that was the problem. His phone vibrated, rattling on the desk almost as loud as the phone call had been. He picked it up quickly and read the message.

*Want 2 go out 2nite?*

Harry looked at his computer screen, the traitorous spreadsheet seemingly mocking him, then typed out his reply.

*Yes.*

He didn't know what was going on but he knew it wasn't good, and he needed to cast this worry off into the night as soon as possible.

TWO FLOORS ABOVE Harry, in the considerably nicer space that housed the heads of department, Josh Adam Spencer stood at his window and gazed out at his incredible view of downtown, as he liked to do when he was feeling masterful.

Josh had made the unlikely move *from* Australia to New Zealand for work, and had done pretty well for himself, he thought. At only thirty-four years old he was the head of Human Resources for the New Zealand branch of a mid-sized international company, and the youngest head of department in the organisation's history. Josh considered his success to be because, at least in part, he was a good guy who had the balls to *tell it like it was*. Josh prided himself on being the man you could count on to say the thing that everyone was thinking but no one was saying.

In other words, Josh could be a bit of a jerk.

But he was a jerk in charge of a departmental budget with a surplus, and he'd just decided how it would be spent.

It had been a delightfully serendipitous coincidence that he'd been in Symonds Street today at all. He'd been taking a call before a meeting when the most beautiful creature he'd seen in real life walked past him. He'd watched her, captivated, as she stopped to adjust her bag, get a pebble out of her shoe, lose her balance and put a bare foot on the pavement to steady herself, grimace as she replaced the shoe, then straighten and turn abruptly into a doorway. As she started to ascend the narrow staircase between two buildings Josh had jolted into action and followed her up. He'd moved slowly, taking care to tread quietly, aware that he had no idea what lay ahead of him.

At the top of the staircase he cast his eyes around to see three office doors. Luckily, only one of them had a light on and he was able to read, without having to move any closer, the sign on the window: *S & S Investigations*. There'd been a sudden movement behind the door and he'd quickly descended the stairs, breathing hard with both exertion and excitement. As soon as he'd returned to his office he'd shut the door and opened up a search engine. Would he be lucky enough to find her straight away? He was. There, on the main page of the S & S Investigations website was Dr Sophie Swanephol, the co-founder of the agency.

And she was remarkable.

Her unexpectedly blue eyes seemed to look directly into his soul and her dark hair tumbled round her shoulders, framing her perfect face. She looked wistful, vulnerable. Like she had problems that he could solve. Like she needed to be a rescued and he would be her rescuer.

It had then taken him only twenty minutes to come up with a reason to hire S & S Investigations and it was quite brilliant, he thought. He would implement a psychometric testing programme for new hires. Organisations did it all the time. They should already be doing it, really, regardless of Sophie, Josh mused.

But was it enough, Josh pondered as he moved away from the window to return to his desk. It would get his foot in Sophie's door, but what if she needed a bit of time to succumb to his charms? Josh opened up the company's intranet and tapped a few keys on his desktop computer.

He saw with disappointment that they did not currently have any vacant positions to fill. But perhaps, he sat up, excited with the idea that had just come to him, perhaps he could integrate some aspect of psychometric testing into the corporate restructure they were about to announce. Yes. The guys upstairs would be on board with a way to shuffle people around and streamline operations. It was perfect. And he would get to work alongside her for weeks, if not months. He stared at Sophie's photo again, getting lost in her eyes. This enchanting creature, this *angel*, was bound to fall for him by then.

SOPHIE LET OUT a little burp, then pushed her tongue around her back left molars.

There was something stuck back there. She opened the top drawer of her desk and eyed the bag of trail mix inside. It was supposed to be good for keeping blood sugars balanced, but if Sophie was honest with herself she couldn't stand the taste, and its tendency to get stuck in her teeth was more than a little off-putting. She shut the drawer with a sigh and continued prodding at the alien object for another minute before giving up and resolving to deal with it later tonight with dental floss. After turning her attention back to her computer and her half-completed crossword, Sophie saw the page was now unresponsive. She checked the internet icon. There was an angry red cross.

"Paige?" Sophie craned her neck so that she could see where Paige was sitting in S & S Investigation's second office. It was supposed to be a meeting room for clients, but it had become where they ate lunch, chatted about TV shows, and sometimes took naps on the basic two-seater couch they'd recently purchased from TradeMe. Right now though, Paige had a newspaper spread out on the table and was looking for articles that had the potential to be turned into cases. When Sophie had asked Paige why she didn't look online—her laptop was right beside her—Paige had mumbled something about there being more in the print newspaper; but Sophie knew that Paige wanted to do it this way because it made her feel more like a private investigator.

It was four months ago now that Paige Garnet, tenacious and confident to the point of occasional delusion, had convinced the naturally cautious and more realistic Sophie Swanephol that they should open S & S Investigations. The agency name came from a faintly ridiculous premise—in grad school Paige and Sophie had been known as *Squirrel and Swan*—but they could claim rather impressive psychological expertise: Paige understood the mechanics of the mind and Sophie could read human behaviour like a book. Plus, according to Paige at least, they made the perfect detective duo, because no one noticed Paige but everyone noticed Sophie.

Despite Paige's assurances and their recent successes—*The Case of the Remuera Pet Napper* and *The Disappearance of Polly Dixon*—however, Sophie still felt fraudulent calling herself an actual investigator. Nonetheless, she allowed Paige's confidence to propel her through the might of her own doubt. At least, she had so far. And there wasn't anything else that Sophie could imagine doing. The alternatives of either returning to the fraught world of academia, or venturing into a new, foreign environment, were equally distasteful.

Sophie eyed Paige, currently drumming her fingers loudly on the table as well as jiggling both her knees, then repeated, "Paige? Can you access the internet?"

Paige stood up abruptly then bobbed down to check her laptop. She tsked with irritation. "Nope." She darted back to the main office and jiggled from foot to foot as she picked up the Wi-Fi modem. "I'll try re-setting it."

Sophie suppressed a smile as she watched her friend, now wiggling her bottom slightly. "Do you need to go to the toilet or have you had too much coffee?"

"Neither... Both."

It was Paige's appearance—large, almond-shaped brown eyes, frizzy brown hair, and a small, rather twitchy physique—that had initiated the *squirrel* moniker, and Sophie, being an obvious beauty and with Swanephol as her surname, was of course the *swan*, despite her being anything but graceful.

Sophie returned her gaze to check the internet icon. Despite a few optimistic flashes and beeps from the modem, the red cross remained. "I wonder if it's just us, or the whole building."

"Okay, I'll go to the loo then go downstairs and ask," Paige said, scampering toward the door. "Ooh. There's a light on in 2C." She looked back to Sophie with excitement. "Someone must have rented that place."

So far, S & S Investigations had been the only tenants in the second floor of this heritage building in Symonds Street. It was only a stone's throw from downtown, but this city-fringe suburb had more than its share of vacant buildings, and the area had the distinct air of a small business that could go under at any moment—much like S & S. Their office was a little dusty and dingy, and at the very least needed a fresh coat of paint if not a complete design overhaul, but it suited their imaginings of a detective agency perfectly. There was even a neon sign from a nearby building casting its light inside to complete the whole detective noir vibe, and sometimes Paige would stay there until it got dark so she could enjoy how authentic she felt with neon flickering across her desk.

Sophie's cell phone rang. She eyed the display warily. "It's a private number."

Paige watched Sophie blinking nervously at her phone. "Soph, we're trying to run a business, you can't ignore phone calls, no matter how much they scare you."

"I'm not scared," Sophie said, but didn't move.

"Answer it. I'll see who's in that office and ask if they're having internet issues."

"Fine," Sophie said, biting her lip.

As Paige exited the single-stall bathroom, a familiar but unexpected sound floated across the landing. Was that a piano she could hear?

Paige continued past the door of 2B—the vacant office at the top of the stairs—and stopped outside 2C, the office directly across the stairwell where inside, someone was most definitely stroking ivories. She peered through the unmarked mottled window and could make out a desk facing the door and a couch against the wall to the left, the mirror of where her own desk was, upon which a fuscia blob with blonde hair waited for whoever was butchering Chopin in the other room.

Abruptly, the music stopped and was replaced by faint sounds of murmuring. Then in a flurry of activity, the door opened and a woman, clutching a somewhat defeated-looking child, walked straight past Paige toward the stairs.

"Can I help you?" a voice said from somewhere behind Paige.

Paige turned to find herself facing a woman in her seventies. She had brown hair cut to just below her ears, and bright hazel eyes.

"Oh, Hi. I'm Paige, uh, Dr Garnet, from 2A. Our internet has gone down. I was going to see if you... but..."

The woman raised one eyebrow until it made an impressive arc above her eye and regarded Paige knowingly. "But since I'm old, I couldn't possibly be able to help with something to do with the internet?" she finished.

Paige opened and then closed her mouth. Yes, exactly, but weren't old ladies supposed to be nice? As sweet as custard? Although, the more she looked at this woman, she doubted *old lady* was an appropriate description, despite what her birth certificate might say.

"The younger generation, honestly, the arrogance of you," she continued, but then said, "Never mind." She waved her hand. "If I let all the indignities that people my age suffer bother me, I'd never get anything done." She opened the door wider. "Come inside and let's have a look. I haven't been online today—I haven't even had a chance to stop for lunch. I'm Hazel, by the way."

Paige followed her inside. "You teach piano?" she asked, poking her head (uninvited) into the second room and finding that it housed a piano, a couple of chairs, and two large pot plants.

"No, I'm a nuclear physicist," Hazel replied, leaning over the PC on her desk.

Paige snorted. She was beginning to rather like this woman.

She continued to wander around the space, noting that it was a mirror of their own office. In the corner where Paige and Sophie had their beloved coffee machine, Hazel had a blender, a kettle, and a mini fridge. Ooh, a mini fridge, Paige thought, making a mental note. Summer was just around the corner. On the small bench next to the sink the ingredients for a smoothie patiently awaited blending. A packet of protein powder, chia seeds, something green (kale, Paige suspected), and berries. Paige shuddered. How did people drink that stuff? Sophie intermittently would arrive at the office armed with similar supplies for some sort of cleanse, but it never lasted very long.

"My lunch. Every day, if possible. It keeps me young, healthy and trim," Hazel said, noting the direction of Paige's attention. "Studies have shown that being thin extends your lifespan."

"Mainly experimental work with animals though," Paige said.

Hazel eyed Paige, seeming impressed. "Perhaps, but it has worked for me."

"You weren't here when we set up our office," Paige said, finishing her tour of nosiness at Hazel's desk. "But it doesn't look like you've just moved in." While it was tidy, the office looked very much like it had been here for a while.

"I've been teaching piano here for years, but for the last few months I've been away."

"And they let you keep the lease? Or did you pay rent while you were away?"

Hazel straightened and regarded Paige for a moment, seeming to consider whether or not to indulge her nosy questions. "I own the building," she said finally.

"How did you manage that? Did you inherit?"

"Do I not seem capable of owning property myself?"

"I just thought…"

But before Paige could offend her with the reasoning behind her curiosity, Hazel answered her question.

"My sister and I inherited money from our parents and… well, it's a long story but John and I made a good investment in the eighties… and from there we had the capital to purchase further properties. Such as this one. John passed away several years back, so now this is my retirement plan."

Paige nodded. "Right. Well, I'm your tenant."

Hazel's mildly irritated expression suddenly turned into a smile. "Yes. The investigations agency. I was rather surprised when the property manager told me about you. Or, impressed, I should say. An unusual endeavour for two young women... And I know first-hand how challenging it can be to open your own business, so... Good on you. In my opinion there aren't enough women going into business for themselves." She nodded. "I can already tell you're made of the right stuff to succeed."

Paige's chest felt weirdly tight. Even with her seemingly endless optimism, she could admit to herself that all this hadn't been particularly easy, and it often felt like the whole world was waiting for her to fail. Hazel was possibly the first person to congratulate her.

She gulped. "Um. Thank you."

"And since the renovations might be a little disruptive, I'm giving you a short-term decrease in the rent."

"Great!" Paige beamed. "Wait, what renovations?"

"Simone didn't tell you?" Hazel tsked. "I'm going to fix a few things here and there. Spruce it up a bit."

"Why now? You're not selling it are you?"

Hazel eyed her for a moment. "I'm not sure yet."

Paige folded her arms. She *loved* their office.

"Don't worry, even if I did sell, I can build in your tenancy with the sale. It's usually more attractive to buyers. It's a historic building so it's not as if they can tear it down," Hazel added, anticipating Paige's next question. Her eyes flicked down to her computer then back to Paige. "My internet is working fine," she added. "You'll have to call your provider." Hazel raised her eyebrows. "Okay?" She moved away from the desk and walked toward the second room, seeming to be dismissing Paige, but then suddenly said, "Wait. You're an investigator in the normal sense, correct? You investigate—"

"Anything, really." Paige was reluctant to mention their first case had been to locate a missing cat. She eyed Hazel. "Why, do you need—?"

"Perhaps, yes. I may need to hire you. I'll get back to you," she said mysteriously.

Paige grinned. A potential new case, just like that.

WHEN SOPHIE ENDED the call she paused for a moment, resisting the urge to clap her hands with excitement. Wanting to find Paige to tell her the good news, she stood quickly and clumsily, hitting the edge of the desk with her hip and knocking her phone to the floor. It clattered noisily as it slid under the desk.

"Dammit." She crouched down and tentatively groped along the dusty floor under the desk, hoping her hand wouldn't land on anything other than a metal oblong object.

"Sophie?"

She jerked upright, smacking the back of head on the underside of the desk.

"Ow!"

"Christ, are you alright?"

Sophie straightened slowly, blinking to clear the spots in front of her eyes as she continued to rub the back of her head. But when she saw who was there, she jerked completely upright. "Roman!"

Roman Leconte, a respected detective in the Auckland city police department, had come to be known to S & S Investigations when he had also been involved the case of the missing Polly Dixon. Since then, Sophie had tried and failed to come up with both a reason and the nerve to contact Roman, but here he was, right in front of her.

He smiled, that crooked half-smile of his, with one side of his mouth tugging up, eventually pulling a seemingly reluctant other side up too.

"Are you okay?"

"Oh, yes. Fine." Sophie blushed and raised her hand to her cheek, then dropped it down and, just for something to do, picked up the cup of coffee in front of her. Forgetting it'd gone cold she took a large mouthful and immediately grimaced, holding the unpleasant liquid in her mouth indecisively until her eyes started to water. Finally, she made the inexplicable decision to raise the cup to her mouth again and eject the coffee slowly back into the cup.

Roman watched her, his eyebrows creased together as his smile threatened to erupt into laughter. Sophie set down the cup and waved her hand, as if to say she was fine, and tried to tuck her hair behind her ear, before remembering it was pulled up in a high ponytail.

"How are you?" she said finally, meeting his eyes. In that moment of connection time seemed to suspend—for just a second—and then Sophie smiled, a spontaneous and completely genuine grin that she didn't seem to have control over.

Why did she feel like she'd been inhaling adhesives whenever he was around?

"I'm good, thanks," Roman replied.

A pinkish hue was spreading across his neck. Sophie, noticing this, felt her own cheeks warm. She'd been a little dumbstruck from the moment she'd met Roman, but it wasn't that he was incredibly good-looking or anything—although he was attractive, with olive skin, brown button eyes, and close-cropped brown hair. It was his solid, reassuring presence, his kindness, and the way he was so calmly masterful. He seemed to be a real *man*, capable of doing actual *stuff*, and made everyone else she'd ever dated suddenly seem like immature boys. In fact, they mostly were. Sophie tended to make poor choices in this department—her intelligence and her behavioural analysis skills did not seem to extend to her romantic life—so her crush on Roman was somewhat of an exception.

Roman cleared his throat. "I, uh," he paused, looking around the office. "Is Paige out?"

"She's just across the hall," Sophie said, trying to ignore the flip-flopping of her stomach. Roman wanted to see her alone?

"Ah." Roman dropped his voice. "I wanted to talk to you about her father."

Sophie nodded, letting the flames of her desire abate at the mention of the death of Paige's dad. Terry Garnet had died during a fishing trip four years ago, and while it was considered a cut and dried accident, during the wrap-up of the Polly Dixon case Roman had told Sophie he wasn't altogether convinced of this. But Paige and her father had been very close, and even now she was still grieving for him, so mentioning this suspicion to Paige and potentially opening up the wound of his death was not something Sophie would do without good reason.

Roman's phone rang. He glanced at it then sent the call to voicemail. "Maybe we could grab a coffee some time? I'm going to have a look at the old case files and see what I can find. We can go over things once I've done that? Just you and me… obviously."

Sophie's stomach flipped again. "Okay."

Roman nodded. "So... you're interested in, uh, helping me figure this out?" He lifted his left hand and scratched his head.

Sophie noticed, again, the slight indent where a wedding ring used to be. He clearly had been married—recently enough to have a mark—but how long ago?

Was Roman bouncing around in rebound city?

"Yes, I am." Sophie nodded firmly. Of this she was completely certain. "Text me?" she added, handing him one of the business cards she had on her desk.

Roman took it and smiled. "Great. I'll be in touch."

Sophie watched as he turned to leave, noting the way his jacket bunched a little around the tops of his arms and upper back, and his trousers seemed a little snug around his backside. Once she was sure he had gone, Sophie closed the office door and returned to her computer. Then, unable to contain the surge of happiness pushing up through her chest, put on CeCe Peniston's classic nineties song *Finally* and turned it up as loud as it could go. Sophie twirled and gyrated and shimmied with abandon until she tripped on her laptop cord, staggered across the room and knocked over the pot plant.

Paige opened the door. "Sophie, *what* are you doing?"

"Nothing, whatever." Sophie gave Paige a sheepish smile as she dusted the soil from her hands. "Guess what? That phone call I took might be a new client."

# 2

Paige and Sophie took seats at one of the empty tables on the far side of Galbraith's, the pub across the road. This mid-week catch-up—the Wednesday Wine & Whine—had begun during their PhD studies, and even though they had less to complain about now that they were their own bosses and didn't have supervisors on their backs and deadlines stressing them out, they'd recently decided to resurrect the ritual.

Galbraith's looked like a traditional English pub but served gastro-pub type food and drinks at Auckland prices—patrons of local pubs in the UK would have been horrified at what people paid for a pint—and though it wasn't really Paige or Sophie's normal style, it was convenient, and their triple-cooked fries were virtually irresistible.

"Okay," Paige said, returning to their table in the corner with a glass of red wine for each of them. "Tell me about the new client."

"The call was from this guy Josh Spencer, and it's a corporate job. They want psychometric testing."

This was one of the services they'd listed on the S & S website, along with everything else short of changing lightbulbs—neither Sophie nor Paige were willing to put their hand up for such a practical task. They weren't specialists in this area, but Paige thought that between the two of them they were certainly capable of conducting a few tests.

Sophie gave Paige a rundown of her conversation as Paige nodded enthusiastically. Working in a corporate environment was a different kind of gig, but it was worth a lot of money, and while their bank account was looking healthy at the moment, it wouldn't last long.

"So," Paige said once Sophie had finished. "What is it, exactly."

Sophie looked at Paige in alarm.

"I mean, I know what psychometric testing is in general, but do you know what actual tests we would administer?"

"Working on it," Sophie said. "I already downloaded some stuff. I had to buy a programme... software... but it wasn't very expensive," she paused, checking that Paige wasn't reacting badly, "and if this goes well, this could become, like, our bread and butter. Our Cash Cow, so to speak."

Sophie had taken a couple of marketing papers early in her undergraduate degree and she'd hated them with a passion, but for some reason she'd been unable to shake such key marketing terms from her long-term memory.

"I am one hundred percent on board," Paige said. "We can use jobs like this to pay all our bills, and then we have the financial freedom to investigate more exciting cases when they come up."

Paige had watched almost every detective or private investigator movie and TV show ever made and the agency she'd envisaged was definitely less corporate and more detective noir.

"When's the meeting?" Paige asked.

"Friday, three o'clock. It's in the S & S calendar." Sophie hadn't needed to check with Paige before setting this up. Not only did they have a shared Google calendar, they currently had zero other clients or commitments. After the successful completion of their first two cases, they hadn't been as inundated with work as they had hoped.

"And you said you might have a lead as well?" Sophie said.

Paige told Sophie about Hazel, their new neighbour, then added, "It's only a maybe—she was reluctant to talk about it—but she said she'd come and chat to us when she was certain she wanted to go down that route. Her words."

Sophie nodded. "But still exciting to possibly have two new clients at the same time. We might finally be able to pay Leo to do something."

Leo was their IT consultant (AKA hacker for hire), an arrangement that had been set up after he was revealed by Paige to be the Remuera Pet Napper. Paige had let him off the hook because she'd immediately recognised the potential value of his computer skills for investigations. Especially if he was prepared to engage in some less-than-totally-legal activities. Leo, swinging in the breeze a bit and having already taken a real shine to both Paige and Sophie, had jumped at the opportunity to work with them.

"I can't imagine we're going to need him on a corporate job," Paige said. "But maybe for whatever Hazel wants us to do."

"Yeah. I feel bad we still can't offer him any paid work."

"He's still working at the DVD rental store, so that will pay his rent, right?"

For the past six years Leo had worked part time at an indie DVD and video rental store in Dominion Road. That such a rental store was still in business was somewhat incredible, but there seemed to be enough people around who liked that sort of thing to support its continued existence.

Sophie shrugged. "How much could that possibly pay?"


LEO, IN FACT, was totally skint, and as a last resort—short of asking his parents for another 'bridging loan'—was currently in the process of asking his high school friend Barrett to help him out.

Barrett was doing pretty well for himself, at least, compared to Leo. He was making good coin in his job as a junior analyst and had virtually no expenses to speak of because Barrett was the stereotypical gamer nerd, living off the spoils of his parents in their basement while indulging in an unhealthy obsession with the female characters (and a couple of the male ones, Leo had noticed), in World of Warcraft.

"What do you say, Bar?" Leo said, aware his voice sounded weird. He was trying for a blokey tone but he didn't seem entirely in control of his voice-box. "You've got some spare cash, don't you?"

"Affirmative," Barrett said, keeping his eyes fixed on the computer screen.

Leo waited, watching Barrett's thumbs move on the controller with incredible agility. Even in the absence of any outward indication, such as a facial expression or even a gesture, Leo could tell Barrett was enjoying this.

"I do, in fact, have some extra cash-ola," Barrett intoned, his eyes still on the screen.

"Uh-huh?" Leo said hopefully, but Barrett did not speak for another couple of minutes until finally, he turned to face Leo.

"I'll hook you up," he said, lifting his chin and squinting at Leo, trying to seem cool and nonchalant, or like some sort of gangster, Leo thought. He sometimes wondered why he and Barrett were still friends. He could be such a dork.

"Great. Awesome, thanks." Leo, his palms still sweaty from the tense exchange, stood up, wiping his hands on the legs of his jeans. "I'd better get going. So, can we meet up soon to sort it?"

Barrett eyed Leo, holding the moment for longer than necessary, then nodded.

Leo left with a sinking feeling in his stomach. Barrett had clearly loved wielding that power, even for a short amount of time, which didn't bode well for his behaviour once Leo owed him money, but what choice did he have?


AFTER SAYING GOODNIGHT to Sophie, Paige did not go directly home to the Mt Albert bungalow she shared with her partner Tim, she instead went to see her mother, with whom she was somewhat surprisingly enjoying a bit of a détente—a hiatus from their normally antagonistic relationship.

"Mum?" Paige called.

The house was quiet.

Paige moved through the large villa, eventually finding her mother in the back garden, attacking what Paige could only assume were weeds. Alice was sweating, rather profusely, Paige noticed, something she wasn't sure she'd ever seen her do before. Alice presented as a small, contained, and immaculately groomed package, and Paige could understand why Sophie had confessed—after a few wines—that she couldn't imagine Paige's mother ever producing any sort of bodily emission.

"Oh, Hello. Did you need something?" Alice sat back on her heels and pulled off her gardening gloves. She glanced briefly at the darkening sky as she stood up. "It really is getting a little out of control," she said, waving her hand at the garden. "I think I'm going to have to employ someone to help."

Paige followed her mother back into the kitchen and hovered at the counter while Alice washed her hands and retrieved a bag of fresh *Homestyle Chicken* soup from the fridge. "Oh," Alice paused, "are you here for dinner? We could make this work for two with a bit of a bread and a salad."

But Paige remained silent, standing near the counter, struck by how solitary this scene was. She turned to take in the living room, suddenly acutely aware of the large emptiness of this house.

Was her mother lonely?

"What's wrong?" Alice said.

"Uh, nothing..." Despite their recent friendliness, Paige didn't want to ask if her mother was suffering from loneliness. Good lord—what if she wanted to live with her and Tim?

"You know... stuff," Paige added, waving her hand dismissively. "S & S stuff."

"Mm-hmm." Alice offered a tight-lipped smile.

Paige's mother hadn't shown much interest in her doctoral studies, but now that she was pursuing the investigations business, Paige thought her mother was probably wishing she would return to the relative prestige of academia. And as much as S & S Investigations was a way for Paige to feel closer to her father, it was also a way to irritate her mother.

"And what about that business with Richard?" Alice asked.

"Oh, uh..."

Paige's relationship with her doctoral supervisor had been uncomplicated... until she graduated. Now, they seemed to be progressing toward becoming arch nemeses at a healthy clip.

"He's away. There's a bunch of data I gathered that hasn't been analysed yet and he wants to write a paper or two, but that will have to wait until he gets back."

"Can't you do it without him?"

"I think he wants to do it without *me*."

Richard had emailed to say he was off overseas, and the way he'd phrased his comments about the data had set off alarm bells for Paige. Even though she'd left academia and was firmly committed to S & S, there was no way she'd let him cut her out of the accolades she deserved. And any such accolades could be used to get traction for S & S. If she was a famous memory expert, people might start flocking to their doors, happy to pay handsomely for her expertise.

"Well, then." Alice held up the soup. "So that's a no for dinner? You're sure?"

Paige shook her head. "Sorry, I've got to dash, Tim's already got dinner on."

"How nice for you."

As Paige waved goodbye and turned away she suppressed both an eye-roll and a little flicker of guilt.

SOPHIE LET HERSELF into the airy and beach-handy Pt Chevalier cottage she shared with her flatmates Victoria and Myra and kicked off her shoes at the door. She moved past her bedroom down the hall to the living room.

"Hey," Victoria said, tossing her long blonde hair over her shoulder and grabbing the TV remote, giving Sophie a small smile as she clutched it to her chest, as a three-year-old might do when they realise they could be forced to share their toys.

Sophie managed a tight smile in return, hovering in the living room as she ran an internal check to see whether she was up to hanging out with her flatmates this evening.

"So, the landlord is coming by next week," Victoria announced into the silence. "The letter is on the table. She wanted to come on Friday, but I got her to switch it. I thought it was appropriate, being the lease-holder and all." Victoria's expression was both knowing and beneficent.

Victoria held the lease to the flat and she liked to remind Sophie and Myra of this on a regular basis, as if it was such an arduous and onerous task of which only she was capable, and in carrying it out, she should be afforded many privileges and rights. Not to mention Victoria was of the opinion that she, at the ripe old age of thirty-one and a (self-described) PR maven, was the utmost authority on any subject you could throw at her.

"What for?" Sophie's stomach clenched. She, as much as Victoria could be insufferable, liked living there, and the thought of having to find another flat was rather horrendous. And since Victoria had lived there for so long and the owners were a hands-off elderly couple, they hadn't had a rent increase in years. The amount Sophie was paying was by far all she could afford with her meagre S & S income.

Victoria shook her head and frowned, as if asking about the purpose of the visit would have been well and truly beside the point.

"Okay," Sophie said. "I guess we'll find out." She tried to push away the bulb of anxiety. There was no point in worrying about something until it had happened, she told herself firmly. She was determined to stop imagining the worst possible outcome for every event. This catastrophizing had the potential to engulf her entire personality.

"Hi, Myra," she said, turning to notice her other flatmate floating near the kitchen door, giving the impression that she might not be able to cross the threshold.

"Hi," Myra replied quietly, still hovering as if waiting to see what Sophie was going to do. Myra was shy and sweet and tended to keep to the shadows, listening and observing as if trying to learn the ways of the 'big girls' living in the 'big city'. One would've thought this would be an ideal flatmate for Sophie, but all that sifting around could get pretty annoying.

"I'm watching Queer Eye," Victoria announced firmly, obviously concerned one of them would try to—heaven forbid—watch something of her own choice on the shared TV. "Unless you were thinking movie night?" She said, her voice suddenly turning hopeful.

"No, I'm going to watch something in my room," Sophie said.

Sophie wanted to be alone. She wanted to watch the finale of Offspring without interruption, but most of all... she wanted to think about Roman.

## 3

Josh Spencer was over six feet tall, with a head full of dark hair and symmetrical facial features. From a distance he checked the 'tall, dark and handsome' box but close up, Sophie discovered, each of his features were slightly too large to produce conventional beauty. Plus, he had the unbecoming tendency to deliver smirks instead of genuine smiles, and upon meeting him Sophie's first instinct was to take a step away. This instinct she resisted. He was in charge of the HR department, so even though he was a little smarmy, he was obviously good at his job—or good at something that led to success.

"Sorry," Sophie said after the introductions had been made and she had extracted her hand from his lingering grip. "Paige, uh, Dr Garnet is uh... tied up with another client. She'll join us presently." Sophie hoped this was true. She had not envisioned making this pitch by herself and the thought sent her sympathetic nervous system into overdrive.

They'd gotten all the way downtown, nice and early for their three o'clock appointment, and were less than twenty feet from their destination when a man carrying a gigantic cup of coffee had barrelled into Paige, knocking her completely off her feet and spilling his coffee all over her shirt. The man had been too busy staring at Sophie to notice Paige marching along beside her, but he certainly noticed her after the string of expletives that Paige had directed at him.

After he'd backed away, apologising profusely, Paige and Sophie had stared at each other in horror. Paige was literally dripping in coffee.

"What should we do?" Sophie said.

"I have a change of clothes at the office."

"You do?" Sophie said, impressed and thinking she should do that same. People didn't bang into her with the frequency they did Paige, but she'd caused more than her share of human fender benders and she'd certainly spilled food and beverages on herself enough times to warrant keeping a clean outfit or two at the office.

"Yep." Paige didn't add that the reason was because she'd seen this in a number of a PI movies—after working an all-nighter the private dick would pull out a fresh shirt and start his day. "I'll be back in time," Paige had promised, beetling away at top speed.

Sophie had watched her go, nervousness already washing over her shoulders. It wasn't possible to get all the way up town and back down again in fifteen minutes, was it?

"Sophie?" Josh said. "Let's go up. I'm sure we can manage on our own until your colleague gets here."


PAIGE HAD JUST thrown on a fresh shirt—her skirt was dark blue and only slightly damp—and was about to leave the office when someone cried out in the hallway.

"Oh!"

The voice was clearly distressed so Paige quickly moved out to the landing area at the top of the stairs. Hazel was standing outside her office, looking in the direction of the darkened hallway.

"Is someone there?" she called, then without waiting for a response, "did you hear that?"

"Hazel?" Paige said. "Are you talking to me?"

But instead of replying, Hazel looked around wildly then abruptly disappeared into her office, only to emerge again a moment later with a set of keys. Paige watched her go over to 2B, the office at the top of the stairs, and unlock the door. She disappeared inside but returned after only a few moments.

"Oh," she said, seeming to only then notice Paige. "You didn't hear that? The voice?" she asked.

Paige shook her head.

Hazel turned away and muttered in a perplexed voice, "It sounded like my sister."

A second later, she'd disappeared inside her own office.

Paige stared after her.

That was weird.

After a moment's indecision, Paige followed Hazel into her office.

"Hello?" she called as she moved past the front desk and into the second room that housed the piano. She found Hazel sitting in the dimly lit room in front of the piano, with a strangely blank expression on her face.

"Hazel? Are you...?" Paige looked around for a student. "What are you doing?"

Hazel swivelled her head toward Paige slowly and frowned. "You're not supposed to be here," she said.

"I saw the door open and..." Paige trailed off.

Hazel's frown deepened. "Did you want a lesson?"

"What? A lesson? Uh, no. I, uh, Hazel. It's me, Paige. From across the hall."

An awful sensation was crawling over Paige's skin.

Hazel blinked. "Yes, oh. Um. Sorry. Not now."

Paige stared at Hazel, unsure what to do.

Silence descended on the small room, making Paige feel almost claustrophobic.

"It was my sister," Hazel said into the silence.

"What was?" Paige said.

"The voice." She pointed across the room. "I'm sure of it."

Suddenly Hazel looked wary. "I think you should leave."

"Um, okay."

Taking slow steps, Paige exited Hazel's office. What on earth was all that about?

FIFTEEN MINUTES LATER, as Josh was trying to adjust his chair so that it was closer to Sophie's and Sophie was trying to surreptitiously check her phone for a message from Paige, the door to 14-04, one of the smaller meeting rooms on the fourteenth floor—but still very nice—banged open.

"I'm late," Paige announced rather than apologised. "Dr Garnet. Co-founder of S & S."

How did someone so small generate so much noise, Sophie wondered as her colleague entered the room. She hoped Josh didn't find her aggressive and intrusive. Or at least, so much so that he didn't want to work with them. But Paige could have walked in with a marching band belting out *Pomp and Circumstance* for all Josh noticed. He'd taken the opportunity of Sophie's averted gaze to indulge in some unabashed ogling.

"Let's get started, shall we?" Paige said.

An hour later, Josh leaned back and clasped his hands behind his head. "Well, that's that then. It all sounds great." He beamed at Sophie. "The final decision will be made upstairs, but I'm sure they'll be just as keen on introducing psychometric testing as I am." He sat up again and snapped his fingers. "But I do need you to sign the non-disclosure agreements before we go any further.

Even what we have discussed today is confidential, you realise." Josh opened the leather document holder in front of him and slid a small wad of papers toward Sophie. "You both sign this one. Excuse me while I make a phone call."

Sophie and Paige grinned at each other as Josh left the room, refraining from squealing and high-fiving and instead sensibly focusing on reading the small print.

When Josh returned, Paige said, "All we have to do now is discuss our fee structure."

"Oh, well, I thought we might—"

"Nonsense." Paige cracked her knuckles. "We'll just take care of the financials and then we're good to go."

Sophie smiled to herself. Paige might have the tendency to offend everyone she met, but—Sophie took in Josh's suitably alarmed expression as Paige brought out a calculator—she also could do *this*.

JOSH CHOSE AN ostentatious place in Chancery Lane to take them for a celebratory drink.

The sole reason for scheduling a meeting at three o'clock on a Friday—normally knocking off time—had been so that he could transition the meeting into a drinks situation. When Sophie had shown up alone he'd felt the universe was conspiring with him—it would be just the two of them having a cosy drink together! But even with the unwelcome arrival of her small and annoying colleague, Josh was not ready to say goodbye to Sophie. And so, despite still having to get this entire scheme approved, he insisted on taking them out in anticipation of celebration.

He swaggered in, pretending to be best friends with the Maître D, who pretended right back because he knew how to play the game. The provision of elevated status and the appearance of hotshottedness was paid for via an overpriced menu and the expectation of generous tipping. This system was one that worked well for the restaurant, for people like Josh, and even the poor wait staff who had to put up with this kind of obnoxious charade on a daily basis, because at the end of the night they got the tips. The drunker these types of people, or the more they were trying to show off, the bigger the tip. When Josh strutted in with Sophie on his arm, the Maître D thought *cha-ching*. Sure enough, Josh ordered an expensive bottle of champagne for the table, took a seat on the patio and leaned back as if the surrounding environs had been built at his command.

AN HOUR LATER, Sophie was done. She was one hundred percent *over it*. She'd now had to endure two hours of small talk, business mumbo-jumbo and Josh's fairly constant, albeit subtle, leering. Every time she'd looked down or away, she'd felt his eyes crawling over her face and she'd, quite simply, had enough.

"Well," Sophie said in her best wrapping-up voice. "Thank you so much, Josh," she continued. "For the drinks."

"Don't forget the oysters." Josh smiled.

"And the food. But I really... I have a prior commitment I have to get to," Sophie said as politely as she could.

"Nonsense. We must celebrate. Or don't you want to work with me?" Josh's pouted.

"Oh, um..."

Paige eyed Sophie, who was now looking around with large, almost panicked eyes. "Unfortunately, we *do* have to get going," she stated. "We do not renege on our prior commitments, as you will see once we start working with you." Paige stood up, extending her hand for him to shake.

"Okay, I guess." Josh sulked.

"I'll just use the loo," Paige said, darting away before Sophie could prevent her from leaving.

As Paige scurried away into the recesses of the restaurant, Josh brightened and leaned in to Sophie. "This is going to be great. Working together. You and me." He smiled, but then adjusted his expression to attempt a more brooding one Ryan Gosling was known for.

For a moment Sophie wondered why Josh was squinting at her and wondered whether the oysters were repeating on him, but when he shifted position in his seat and brought his hand up to stroke his jaw, she realised he was trying to look cool.

"Yes. I look forward to it." Sophie stood up and made to leave. She didn't care whether Paige was out of the toilet yet or not. "So, shall I call to follow up on Monday morning?"

Sophie had no intention of making that call herself—phone calls were Paige's department—but it was the right thing to say in the moment.

Josh also stood, seeming to enjoy the way he could tower over her. Sophie was not at all short, but he was still several inches taller.

"Yes. We'll need to clear it with the boys upstairs," he winked, "but with my go-ahead, it'll all be fine. I'll take care of everything," Josh added, his voice dropping a few decibels. "Just give me a few days," he added, leaning down to grip both of her shoulders.

Sophie flinched at this invasion of her personal space. In the distance, she could see Paige's brown hair bobbing toward them so she extracted herself from his grip and extended her hand.

"Thanks again. Have a good weekend." She nodded, backing away before he could say or do anything else.

On the street, Paige beamed at Sophie. "We have a corporate gig!" She raised her hand so that Sophie could high-five her.

Sophie, feeling tension slip away, slapped her hand and grinned.

"What about a martini at The Gin Room?"

"Perfect," Sophie said, following Paige into Vulcan Lane.

JOSH STAYED FOR another fifteen minutes after they'd left. There was still a glass of champagne in the second bottle and while he'd consumed one bottle almost all by himself and was light-headed, he was not ready to go home yet. He would detour past the White Lady for a burger before he drove home, just in case.

Josh knew his promise to get everything sorted by Monday meant he'd be working this weekend, but it was worth it. He'd have to put together a presentation for the aforementioned boys upstairs before this would become an approved part of the corporate restructure. He himself could hire Sophie as an HR initiative within his budget, but if he wanted to have Sophie around on a more regular basis, he needed to get their okay.

He sipped the champagne, letting his mind return to Sophie. He thought about how when they'd stood up she'd looked up at him, her big eyes wide with innocence and a sweetness he could almost smell. How did she manage to make a basic shirt and skirt look so... *intoxicating*. Her hair had been pulled back in a simple ponytail and he had spent the last hour aching to pull it out. Or for her to pull it out herself and then shake out her gorgeous mane of hair. He shifted in his seat. Oh yes. He looked up to find the whereabouts of the waiter and motioned with a languid wave of his hand that he was ready to pay. While he waited he leaned back in his chair and, looking very much like an evil mastermind one might see in a movie, he let out a low, calculating chuckle and rubbed his hands together.

In a few months he'd have everything he wanted.

# 4

Paige growled with irritation.

She loved the Mt Albert bungalow she shared with Tim, with its three bedrooms and a back garden with space for the BBQ and an outdoor dining set. It was perfect, except for one thing. Currently, it was nine o'clock on Saturday morning, sunny but rather chilly, and their neighbours had opened every single door and window in their house for the sole purpose, it seemed, of creating an audience for a morning session of jiggery pokery.

"Honestly, they've got to be doing it on purpose. Every time, I swear."

"For all we know, they're doing it all day and only have the door open sometimes," Tim said.

Paige flicked her eyes across to him, standing at the stovetop making an omelette.

He turned to regard Paige, pushing his glasses up his nose with the back of his hand before returning his attention to the fry pan. "Try not to let it bother you. It's not like it's a P party."

Paige stared at him. "That's pretty much the worst possible neighbour scenario. Things can be bad and not be as bad as that."

He shrugged. "Well, at least they don't have loud arguments all the time."

"Ugh." Paige wanted to stamp her foot. Just once she'd like for him to get mad alongside her. She knew he was right, but his easy-breezy attitude could be annoying.

As Tim served up their breakfast, a delighted shriek pierced the air, followed by giggling.

"Right, that's it," Paige said, setting down her fork.

"Paige, no."

"I'm just going to let them know that we can hear them, okay?"

"Really?" Tim's face reddened in anticipation. "You're going to tell them we can hear them having sex?" he whispered.

"Are you coming with me?"

Tim grimaced, but followed Paige as she marched around to the side of the house, stepped across the line of shrubs that demarcated their properties, and carried on up to the deck and rapped on the glass of their open French doors.

"Hello?" she called.

A minute later, a guy, mid-twenties, wearing shorts and a check shirt, appeared in the hallway. "Hi?" He looked puzzled for a second. "Oh, you're our neighbour, right?" He ambled down the hall toward the door.

Paige nodded. "Listen. We can hear you."

"Hi, mate," Tim said from behind her. "Sorry about the intrusion. We're your neighbours. I'm Tim. This is Paige."

"Craig," he said with a smile before a frown wrinkled his brow. "Sorry, what's that? You can hear us?"

"We thought we should let you know, for your own privacy, really."

Luckily for Tim, the redness of his face adequately conveyed the message and he didn't have to say the actual words. Or listen to Paige say them.

"Ahh, gotcha," Craig said, nodding slowly and putting his hands into his pockets.

"Craig?" A woman, also in her mid-twenties, came to join him at the door. She was wearing a floaty print top, but it didn't disguise the swelling of her stomach.

Paige stared at her for a moment before blurting, "You're pregnant."

"I'm aware of that." She grinned.

"You're too young!" Paige added, not helping the matter.

"I'm twenty-six," she replied, tilting her head. "My mother had me when she was twenty-three."

Tim was now beaming. "How far along are you, if you don't mind me asking?"

"Twenty-nine weeks," she said, rubbing her belly. "Getting close."

"Hey, thanks for letting us know," Craig said. "She gets hot so we open the doors, but... yeah. We'll put the fan on, and, uh, bear that in mind."

"Thanks," Tim said. "That would be great. And congratulations."

Paige nodded, uncharacteristically quiet.

As they walked back across to their house Tim said, "See? People have babies before they're thirty."

Paige didn't know what to say.

VICTORIA BRUSHED HER long blonde hair, admiring the way it glinted in the sun streaming into her room—the largest and most optimally positioned in the house—and wondered whether she should wear it up or down. She was thinking about a side plait, but she got more *looks* when her hair was out. Still in a towel, she moved across to her wardrobe to select the perfect brunch outfit, flicking through hanger after hanger, trying to quell the excitement that was already building.

She loved going places with Sophie.

It was already all imagined in her head. They would get a patio seat at a trendy spot in Ponsonby, she would put on her largest, darkest glasses, and then sit back and enjoy the looks they got as people tried to work out who they were. With her long, expensively dyed blonde hair, her stylish clothes, and the air of disinterested awareness she'd perfected over the years, Victoria could pass as a possible celebrity. Especially if they were in Ponsonby. But it was mostly her companion that generated the interest. Who was Sophie? A movie star they couldn't quite place? A local celebrity, or perhaps a WAG from a local or a visiting team?

This kind of speculation and attention, of which Sophie was excruciatingly aware and tried to avoid, was one of the reasons Sophie hated going to brunch—at least at the kind of place Victoria would pick. But she couldn't tolerate any more of Victoria's passive aggressive comments and wanted to get back on her good side. Victoria had only just forgiven Sophie for having an unauthorised guest while she was away last month, and only because Sophie had taken her to brunch last weekend. When Victoria had insisted on a second brunch this weekend, saying it was her turn and she simply *had* to return the favour, Sophie knew this was part of her punishment.

When Victoria finally emerged triumphantly from her room ready for their brunch date, Sophie was waiting in the hall wearing *activewear*. Victoria's initial look of disdain turned into one of uncertainty. Activewear was a *look*, after all. Had she completely missed the mark by going for a flirty summer dress and platform wedges?

"Shall we go?" Sophie said brightly, noticing the look on Victoria's face and not wanting to give her a chance to say she had to change, thereby delaying their outing and the time when Sophie could retreat to her room to watch TV and think about Roman without interruption or distraction.

"Uh, sure," Victoria said.

Myra hovered hopefully in the doorway as they fussed with keys and bags, but Victoria had no intention of Myra diluting the impact the two of them had. Not with her unassuming manner and nondescript clothes.

"Don't wait up," Victoria said cheerfully to Myra, which was both mean and inappropriate, given how much Myra wanted to come, not to mention that it was only eleven o'clock in the morning.


PROFESSOR RICHARD THINTON, clad from neck to knees in purple Lycra, eased his bicycle to a stop at the lights at the corner of Ponsonby Road.

Two weeks ago he'd decided to start cycling to work, so he'd purchased one of the most expensive road bikes on the market as well as two completely over-the-top cycling outfits, and he'd joined the other middle-aged male cyclists proudly showing off all their creases and bulges to the unsuspecting commuters who made the unfortunate decision to look out their window while waiting at the lights.

So far the cycling to work had gone well, and Richard rather fancied the way he looked in this cycling gear, so he'd decided to unleash himself onto the weekend population of Ponsonby. He was heading toward the bicycle café in Britomart, but had taken this detour because you never knew who you might run into. Like right now, Richard chuckled to himself as he realised that one of the two attractive girls sitting out on a patio sipping coffee was known to him. When the light went green, he signalled right, turned down Franklin Road, then looped back.

SOPHIE HAD SEEN Richard at the lights—who could have missed him in that outfit?—and was hoping he hadn't seen her. But a minute later, even looking down fixedly at her coffee, Sophie caught Richard's approach out of the corner of her eye.

"Sophie Swanephol, what a pleasure," he said, pulling up in front of them with his bike.

Pleasure wasn't quite the word Sophie would have used. The last time they'd spoken, the conversation had ended on a considerably less friendly tone. Richard had been furious that she'd turned down his offer to work on a project, a Marsden grant no less, and he'd made sure Sophie was aware of his displeasure. Now, however, Richard had either forgotten or chosen to pretend it had never happened.

"Hello, Richard, how are you?" Sophie managed a smile. "I thought you were out of the country at the moment."

"Leaving Monday. Just getting in a last chance for a cycle. New bike," he added proudly, patting the seat.

"I can see that." Sophie said, taking another sip of coffee to give her eyes a rest from the glare of luminescent purple. "All packed then?" she added, for lack of something else to say. She was now regretting her activewear outfit choice, not only because it was relatively figure-hugging, but because she felt as if she and Richard looked like part of some sort of team.

"Hello," Victoria said loudly. "I'm Victoria. Sophie's flatmate."

"Are you indeed? Well then, you two must get up to all sorts of trouble," Richard leered.

Victoria flicked her hair behind her shoulder. "Wouldn't you like to know," she said coyly.

Sophie stared incredulously at Victoria, then turned her gaze to Richard who was grinning back at Victoria. What was happening?

"How do you two know each other?" Victoria continued.

"I'm a professor at the university."

"Oh well, looks *and* brains then," Victoria said. "Your wife is a lucky woman."

Sophie was starting to feel nauseous. "Um. Sorry, just going to pop to the loo," she said, standing quickly and moving inside.

Once away from that awful display Sophie felt better, so she waited, hovering awkwardly near the toilets and enduring the perplexed looks the wait-staff were giving her, until she saw Richard leave, then returned to their table.

"Well isn't he dashing?" Victoria said.

"No, and he's married," Sophie replied.

"I know, I know. But there's no harm in flirting."


MEANWHILE, IN A renovated two-and-a half bedroom cottage in Sandringham, Roman sat in his home office and typed terms into a search engine.

First, the date and location of Terry Garnet's fishing trip, then further searches based on terms like 'fishing', 'currents', 'tides', and finally 'drowning'. Sometimes there was more information to be discovered on the World Wide Web than in their police databases. He hadn't had a chance to look at Terry's official police case file yet, but he suspected that when he pulled it out of archives, there wouldn't be much there.

After he'd downloaded all the news articles that covered Terry Garnet's disappearance and death and saved them into a new folder, he moved on to finding a Coast Guard report for the boating accident. It didn't take long to find a site in which—the internet was a miraculous thing—you could input precise coordinates and dates and get the corresponding weather reports. He copied the information into a document, then saved it to his TG folder, then sat back to take a gulp of coffee.

The front door slammed. Roman looked up and tensed, waiting for his name to be called, but all that floated through to him were the shuffling sounds of shopping bags, so he returned his attention to the screen and carried on with his work.

ABOUT FOUR KILOMETRES away, sitting in his small K' Road apartment, Harry was lighting his first doobie of the day. He relaxed as he exhaled out the window, releasing the smoke to join its cousins in the smoggy air outside.

His existence had over the last year turned into somewhat of a double life. During the week he was a diligent and hardworking payroll clerk, and in the weekend he was a much less conscientious lad who enjoyed recreational drugs. But over time, his weekend persona had started spilling over to his corporate identity, with weekends sometimes beginning on Thursday nights, and only just finishing under an excruciatingly cold shower on Monday morning.

Still, since Harry had done well at university and had a natural affinity with numbers, all signs pointed to a promising career in something in finance. But now this was happening. The discrepancy he'd noticed between the submitted payroll report and the monthly financial report he could neither explain, nor shake from his mind. The whole thing seemed ominous.

It was possible the mistake was on the payroll side, but Kate had prepared the report and this wasn't likely—she was far from sloppy—so Harry now believed the discrepancy wasn't a mistake. He'd attempted to say something to his boss, but ultimately chickened out, instead resolving to speak to Kate first. But she was away on holiday and she wasn't replying to his messages. Not by email, text or social media. Not even when he actually called her. And she'd posted absolutely nothing online in the last week.

A sudden and unpleasant thought barrelled into Harry's consciousness. The two weren't related, were they? Kate taking a holiday at the last minute and this discrepancy? It was possible she'd gone off the grid and was hiking in Nepal or something. But surely she would have said something about such a holiday? He'd known nothing about it. Denise, the office manager, had been the one to tell him Kate was on three weeks leave. Denise had been rather annoyed, it seemed, as her leave forms had come in at the last minute.

And why did he even care about any of this? Why couldn't he just put his head down and do the tasks that were required of him; earn his wage and continue living his life? He never would have pegged himself as being the moral compass for... anything. And yet, here he was, with his internal arrow resolutely pointing to 'wrong' and no clue what to do about it. The pressure was building, slowly but surely.

Harry's abdomen let out a strained squeal, almost whale-like, and he drew one hand in to clasp his midriff and raised the other to take another toke. The shakiness that Harry now felt on a regular basis, the sense that the walls were closing in and that impending doom was just around the corner, was both alleviated and exacerbated by smoking pot. But Harry did not have any other techniques to deal with his recently acquired knowledge, and so he persevered the only way he knew how.

# 5

On Monday, Leo sat at the counter of the DVD and video rental store, under the slightly too bright lights and amongst the aroma of incense which seemed to permanently drift down from upstairs. He eyed Barrett, wondering how much longer he was planning on staying. It was nice to have company and all, but his boss was coming by at some point today, and Barrett was not the sort of friend you wanted your boss to meet. He had *time waster* written all over him. When the door buzzer sounded Leo tensed in anticipation, but it turned out to be Paige.

"Hey." He beamed.

Barrett, who'd been leaning against the counter flicking through a comic book, looked up with interest.

"How's it going?" Paige said to Leo.

"Not bad, you know." He gestured at the customer-less store.

"Is this her? Is this Scully?" Barrett said loudly.

Leo looked at him in disbelief. Barrett was perhaps the most socially clueless individual in the universe—and in the present company that was saying something. It felt like Barrett had used a speakerphone to announce Leo's secret crush to the world.

"It is, isn't it?"

"Cut it out Barrett," Leo hissed, turning an incredible shade of red.

"Hey," Barrett raised his eyebrow and leered, inexpertly, at Paige.

"Sorry," Leo said. "This is Barrett. He says dumb stuff sometimes."

Paige turned to give Barrett her best eyebrow arch.

"What brings you by, Paige?" Leo said, desperate to change the subject.

"I was going to see if you wanted to grab lunch but," Paige gestured at the subway wrapper on the counter, "I can see you've already eaten."

"Yeah," Leo said miserably, mentally sighing. He could have been having lunch with Paige. If only she'd shown up a little earlier. "My boss is coming by today too, so I can't take leave."

"Hey, Scully," Barrett said, either ignoring Leo's earlier comment or not picking up on it at all, "did you know that in phylogeny, the human penis is the largest, relative to body size."

"Really? Tell me," Paige turned her gaze to him. "What species in the phylogenic scale do you use to assess the size of your penis?"

Leo snorted, nearly spilling his Smart Water all over the counter.

One of the perks of working in this kind of anti-establishment environment was that he could eat and drink at his desk. At least that's what Leo thought—the manager of the store was not aware of this particular interpretation of the liberal-edgy ethos he'd set out. If he had been, he would have shut it down immediately.

"So, you don't have any new cases?" Leo asked hopefully.

"Well, we do. Probably. But it's a corporate one. Psychometric testing, personality tests and things like that so..." Paige trailed off, seeming to notice how bummed out Leo seemed. "But there might be another one, we're waiting to see if the lady wants us to, um, do whatever it is she needs doing." Paige waved her hand. "I'll let you know. Anyway, I'm starving so I'm going to get something to eat. See you later, Leo," Paige said as she turned to leave, waving goodbye to the still stunned Barrett.

Once Paige had gone, Leo turned an incredulous face to Barrett.

"Dude. What is wrong with you?"

"What?"

Leo shook his head. Why was he friends with Barrett?

"Hey, I need a favour," Barrett said. "And since, you know…"

Leo sighed. Owing Barrett money was already turning out to be a right pain in the arse.

SOPHIE STOOD AT the corner of New North Road and Symonds Street, casting nervous glances back at the office. Roman had asked her if she was free at one o'clock today and so she'd told Paige she was having lunch with a friend. Even though she'd watched Paige drive away, it still felt risky meeting Roman so close to their building. Because if Paige knew who she was meeting, she would want to know why, and Sophie would have to lie and then it would become a whole thing. It was better to keep it completely on the down-low until Sophie knew whether there was anything to tell.

Sophie checked to her left and right—it was now five past one—and bit her lip. Her armpits were getting sweatier by the second. Just then, seemingly out of nowhere and backlit against the early afternoon sun, Roman appeared, strolling toward her. Sophie raised her hand to shield her eyes from the glare. He was wearing a dark green suit jacket with an open-necked shirt underneath and her chest felt tight just watching him walk over.

When Roman reached her he said, "Hey. Shall we grab a coffee or—"

Sophie's stomach rumbled loudly. She clasped her stomach. "Oh, um."

"I was about to ask if you'd eaten, but you've answered my question." Roman grinned. "Lunch it is. Somewhere nearby?"

"Um, sure."

For a moment they stared at each other, seeming to be unsure as to what to suggest, then in the same instant they abruptly turned and started eyeing their surroundings, as if to consider where they might go. Sophie, feeling as if the mounting pressure of the moment might at any second propel her to say or do something unfathomable, blurted, "What about that place," pointing across the road where a bright-coloured Pirate-themed restaurant sat expectantly on the corner.

"Really? Are you... into Pirates?"

"No, just curious. Do people go there for like, a pirate experience?"

Roman laughed. "Come on, then."

Inside the restaurant a waitress, wearing an off the shoulder puffy white shirt, a bodice, a colourful skirt and an eye patch, appeared in front of them.

"Arr me hearties," she said, bending forward and swinging her elbows back and forth... like a pirate.

Oh wow, Sophie thought. Roman's eyes widened.

"A table for two please," he said with an impressive amount of decorum.

The waitress took two gigantic plastic covered menus from a stash near the door and marched resolutely toward the darkened recesses of the restaurant. There were only a handful of other diners, but she appeared to be heading directly for a table in the back that was equidistant from the door to the toilet and the entrance to the cacophonous kitchen. It was perhaps the worst seat in the house.

"Um, excuse me?" Roman said. "How about this table here." He pointed to a cheerful two-seater table under the window.

The waitress looked uncertain, as if this interruption had completely thrown her off, then shrugged. "No worries," she said, dropping character for a moment to reveal a strong Kiwi accent. As they sat down she placed menus in front of them and patted her waist area, clearly missing a notepad of some sort. "I'll be back in a moment... um... *Arrr.*" She winked unconvincingly as she left.

Roman leaned across the table to whisper, "I think she might be new."

Sophie nodded and picked up the menu. She gave it a cursory glance before peering over the top at Roman. His eyes, peeking over the top of his menu also, met hers briefly and warmed, before a small frown appeared between his brows and he dropped his eyes to the menu. A little curl of uncertainty looped through Sophie's stomach.

Sophie, an expert in behavioural analysis, was usually able to determine at least the general gist of people's thoughts. She could read all the little nonverbal cues: eye twitches, hand gestures, where attention was focussed, the precise moment someone's eyes widened, or their pupils dilated. But in Roman's presence, she found herself having to attend to the much more basic and primal messages shooting around her own system. So, while she felt like some sort of octopus with too many limbs that were not all entirely within her control, she enjoyed that she couldn't easily tell what he was thinking.

The waitress came back. She tilted her head back to regard them, moving her head from side to side so that her unpatched eye could see each of them one at a time. "Ready to order?" she said, now looking down at her notepad, trying to write down the table number but clearly struggling with the effect the eyepatch was having on her depth-perception.

Roman's eyes flicked to Sophie's. His lip twitched. Sophie's eyes widened and she clapped a hand over her mouth to stop a laugh from escaping. They managed to hold on to their composure while they gave their orders, but once she'd retreated they both started laughing, seemingly unable to stop for a good minute.

Finally, still chuckling, Roman reached into his bag and pulled out a manila folder. "Before I forget, I've started looking into Terry's case."

"Yes, of course." Sophie nodded, taking the file from Roman.

In truth, Sophie had almost forgotten this was the reason they were here at all. She flicked through the notes Roman had printed out about tides and currents and weather reports. She was desperately trying to pay attention to the words in front of her, but it was about the weather, after all, and since he had moved closer, she could smell Roman's aftershave. He was wearing the same sandalwood one he'd worn the first time they'd met, but not the day he stopped by the office. Did he have several fragrances he switched between, like women might select earrings or other accessories to go with their outfits or mood?

"So, what do you think?"

"Oh, uh." Sophie put down the papers on the table between the two of them. "Honestly, this kind of thing... I don't know what I'm looking at. Could you...?"

"Of course." Roman smiled. "It basically says that with the currents on the weekend that Terry Garnet went missing, his boat shouldn't have ended up where it was eventually found."

Sophie stared at Roman. "How was this not picked up at the time?"

Roman shook his head. "It seemed to be an accident. But... it's also possible someone messed with or buried the coast guard report. Another reason to suspect foul play." Roman leaned forward a little closer. Sophie could see the flecks of hazel in his eyes and his mouth seemed only inches away. "I've made a start, but we need to gather a lot more than this and I thought if you're not too busy, we could both look into it separately and meet in a week or so to compare notes? If we put our heads together—" Roman broke off awkwardly and pulled back, seeming to realise how close their heads currently were.

Sophie's face felt hot. She hoped it was one of those blushes that only felt hot—that her face wasn't in fact bright red.

Roman cleared his throat. "We might be able to figure this out."

"Sounds good." She managed to make her voice sound even. "I'll have a think about what aspects I can look into, and then hopefully we'll know whether there's anything to tell Paige, without troubling her if there's nothing."

They both nodded their agreement at each other, unable to stop the smiles creeping onto their faces.

PAIGE ANNOUNCED HER return to the office with a slam of the door and the aroma of fried food. Sophie eyed the Burger Fuel takeaway bag but having recently eaten hot chips and calamari herself, she wasn't even jealous.

"You look all pink. You're kind of glowing," Paige said, continuing past but stopping suddenly. "OMG, you're not pregnant are you?"

"What? No!" Sophie replied. "For that to happen I'd need... Let's just say there's a crucial part of the equation missing."

"You're not on Tinder any more, right?"

"No. Taking a break."

"Has that Josh guy called yet about the corporate job?" Paige said, taking a bite of her burger.

Sophie shook her head.

"Should I call him?" Paige asked.

"Not yet. He said he had to get it approved, remember."

"I'll give him until tomorrow."

They both turned back to their laptops, going through emails and notifications. Unfortunately, none of these were related to S & S Investigations or carried even a hint of further work.

"Hey, so," Sophie waved her hand around the office, "Since we have some time we should probably do some cleaning."

Paige wrinkled her nose. "Don't we have money to pay a cleaner? How much could that possibly be?"

"We have enough to pay rent, the loan, and our wages, but not for very long," Sophie reminded Paige. The two cheques they'd received from Carolyn Dixon had been very generous and it had only been a few weeks since they were deposited, but the money was disappearing fast.

Paige made an impatient sound. For all she turned her nose up at wealthy people, she was one herself. She came from a well-off family and was now comfortably living with someone who took care of most, if not all, of the bills. As such, she didn't have the same grasp of economics as someone who had grown up having to count their pennies—and still did.

"We have a mop, floor cleaners, and paper towels, but we need more spray 'n' wipe and glass cleaner, and probably some fly spray for summer, I think." Sophie was making a list. She tapped the pen against her lip. "And some more toilet stuff." Sophie had realised a while ago that the single basic toilet, located down the hall in between 2A and 2B, was not being cleaned. Thankfully it didn't appear to be being used by anyone apart from themselves, although last week when she'd entered the cubicle she'd found the toilet seat up, which was unusual.

"I'll go grab this stuff and come straight back," Sophie said. "Give you a chance to finish lunch," she added to Paige who still had half a burger to eat and the tendency to chew with her mouth open when she was distracted.

At the newly renovated Countdown on the corner of Valley Road, Sophie went straight to the cleaning supplies aisle on the far side. Once she'd picked up the items on her list, she started thinking about what she had in her own fridge for dinner, and wondered whether now was a good time to grab something so she didn't have to do it after work. There was sometimes a loaded air swirling around her local Pt Chev supermarket if you ventured in there after dark. It seemed to be filled with people intent on acquiring more than food items. Plus, if she had food in the fridge, she wouldn't be as tempted by the gauntlet of takeaway outlets she passed on her way home.

Perhaps grilled chicken breast and a Greek salad, Sophie thought, heading toward the meat section. Sophie wished she wasn't one of those people who thought about 'bikini season' and what she ate, but she was. One does not go through high school carrying extra weight without it having a lasting impact. But she tried not to be obsessive or weird about it—living with Victoria she knew first-hand how tiresome someone constantly going on about diets could be.

As Sophie moved toward the vegetable section she spotted a familiar face at the end of the aisle. Simone Baxter, real estate agent extraordinaire. Simone had brokered Paige and Sophie's lease of 2A, but the only recent interaction they'd had with her was when she'd clattered up the stairs to remind them rent was due.

"Oh, you mean *every month* we have to pay rent?" Paige had said. "Gosh, thanks for that life hack, Simone."

Simone had not been impressed by Paige's sarcasm.

Sophie, still watching Simone, realised that the man hovering at her elbow was also familiar to her. He was the guy Sophie and Paige had seen with Simone at Galbraith's a month or two ago. The one who seemed to think he was living behind a two-way mirror; that other people couldn't see who or what he was looking at, and thus felt he could stare at anyone and anything as much as he liked.

Sophie watched as Simone shrugged him off and marched down the aisle in her general direction. Sophie quickly turned and pretended to be looking at the sausage selection until she was sure they both had passed. She had no interest in making small talk with Simone, and her last interaction with that googly-eyed guy had made her feel as if she wanted to take a shower. She peeked over her left shoulder. They were heading for the veges.

"Hey, Babe?" the guy said. "It's Mike as well as Jen tonight, aye? I'll get some beer and what kind of wine do you want?" He spoke loudly, as if to make sure that all the surrounding shoppers were aware that Simone was his living, breathing girlfriend, and they had actual friends who were coming around for dinner.

"I'll pick the wine," Simone muttered, picking up a couple of bags of lettuce and dropping them into her basket.

"Right, right."

"Are you okay for time?" Simone said. She had a mildly pained looked on her face, as if she didn't expect to have to be doing this, right now. Or perhaps, at least not with this guy in tow.

He checked his watch. "Yep. About half an hour, I reckon."

They moved to the alcohol section and Sophie quickly grabbed some lettuce, tomatoes and a capsicum—the avocados were far too expensive—and hurried to the self-service checkout.

AT THE SOUND of the office door opening Paige glanced up.

"Oh, hey, Soph. That was quick—" Paige stopped.

The woman in front of her looked, at least to Paige's eyes, remarkably like Sophie. She had an oval face, golden skin, long dark hair and blue eyes, but unlike Sophie she wore large hoop earrings, had false eyelashes and sculpted eyebrows, and was directing a bored and sulky pout at Paige.

"Barbie Sophie!" Paige blurted.

She smiled, appearing pleased, and used her long fingernails to adjust the hair around her shoulders. "Hannah," she said, casting a seemingly disinterested eye around the office, but actually taking in every detail. Eventually her gaze landed on the business cards sitting on Sophie's desk. She picked one up. "Is she here? Sophie?"

Paige shook her head. "Can I leave a message, tell her you stopped by? Who you are? The reason for your visit? Who you are?"

Hannah slipped the card into the bag slung over her forearm and waggled her fingers at Paige before turning on her platform heels to saunter out. Paige jumped up and scuttled over to the door to watch her descend the stairs.

"There's another Swan," Paige breathed.

TWENTY MINUTES LATER Paige was trying to think of something she could do to delay having to start cleaning with the supplies they already had, when she remembered their neighbour Hazel had said she might need to hire them. She would ignore that weird incident from the other day, Paige decided, and focus on their first meeting. She sprang up excitedly and opened the door to see if Hazel was free to talk.

She didn't have to go very far. Hazel was right there on the landing outside her office, leaning against the edge of the bannister. She leaned further forward, almost hanging over the railing.

"Hazel?" Paige said, watching her with concern. Hazel was a tall woman, and doubled over like that, there was a very real risk that she would topple over and fall the twenty or so feet to the bottom of the stairs below.

Hazel didn't respond but slumped forward another couple of inches. Paige gasped and raced around the landing until she reached her, grasping her by the shoulders and easing her up and away from rail. Hazel was thin, so even as small as Paige was, she was able to support her weight for long enough to get them both back into Hazel's office. She deposited Hazel on the couch near the door and then crouched down in front of her. Hazel was pale and her eyes were cloudy and confused.

"Are you okay?"

"What's happening?"

"I think you might have fainted, or nearly fainted? I found you out on the landing." Paige peered into Hazel's face.

Hazel's brows were knitted together, and for a moment Paige felt sure that Hazel was going to ask who Paige was, but then she cleared her throat and blinked slowly but purposively.

"Yes, I felt faint. I have low blood pressure, and I haven't eaten much today, just my lunchtime smoothie. That must be it."

Paige frowned. Was that all it was? Technically Hazel *was* elderly...

"Is there some water? Please... I'm so thirsty."

Paige hurried over to the kitchenette, found a glass and filled it up. "Here." She held it up to Hazel's mouth. Her skin felt warm and her face was now looking flushed. "What about medications? Have you started a new one that you are reacting to?"

"I don't believe in medicine."

"It exists, I can assure you."

Hazel made an exasperated sound.

What, Paige thought, was Hazel the only one allowed to be sarcastic?

"I don't believe in throwing medicine at every little problem you have," she clarified, her voice sounding clearer. "Nowadays everything is a disease or a disorder, and everyone takes a pill to cure it." Hazel adjusted herself on the couch and sat up a little. "Edward, my nephew, is forever going on about one ailment or another. He takes these concoctions for allergies and I think he's taking pills for depression." She shook her head. "Honestly. He's about as depressed as I am."

Paige agreed that the population was over-medicated in general, but was starting to think Hazel's stance was a tad too harsh. She nodded anyway. "You're feeling a bit better? A bit clearer headed?'

"I'm fine. I'm in perfect health."

People don't nearly faint for no reason, Paige thought.

"Are you sure you're okay?" she said. Hazel nodded. "Okay, well, I'm just across the way so call out if you feel unwell again or need anything." Hazel nodded again but didn't move. "Maybe I should fix you a cup of tea before I go?"

"I'm fine. Really. Just go, please." Hazel waved her off, looking irritated.

Paige backed out of the office and walked back around to S & S.

Even to Paige it was obviously not the right time to ask whether Hazel wanted to hire them, and she wondered whether, no matter how much Hazel insisted she was fine, whether there was in fact something quite wrong.

# 6

The next morning Sophie was standing in Shortland Street, trying to convince herself that she wasn't having a panic attack.

The meeting with Josh was at ten thirty, and like a complete idiot she'd told Paige she didn't need to come.

It was all Victoria's fault.

Well, at least partly. Last night she'd found herself cornered in the kitchen by Victoria, who at first had inundated her with questions about Richard—that silver fox at brunch, in Victoria's words, despite his artfully maintained head of decidedly brown hair—and then continued with an endless barrage of her opinions, loosely presented as conversation. By the time Sophie could escape and stagger to her bedroom she felt as if all the life had been sucked out of her. As she had rubbed her temples to alleviate her Victoria-headache,

Sophie had started to get annoyed. Why couldn't she be more like Paige and say what she thought and state what she wanted? Why couldn't she march around being confidently blunt? Why was she so often engulfed by this kind of anxious fearfulness, whether it was about doing the wrong thing, or saying the wrong thing, or messing up?

Sophie knew most of the reason she was feeling so angsty was this meeting. As soon as Josh had called to let them know when the executives would see them, dread had started creeping into her system, washing over her shoulders and making her feel sick. But she had a PhD in behavioural analysis, for goodness sake. Why was she so nervous? She needed to grab the bull by the horns and make herself face these challenges more frequently, otherwise she'd never overcome her anxiety.

So last night Sophie had resolved to be more assertive and more confident.

Starting with this meeting.

She'd messaged Paige to tell her she'd go to the meeting alone, just to get the contract signed. But now, Sophie couldn't believe she'd been so reckless. Why on earth had she picked now, *this meeting*, to try to get over her self-doubt?

She hadn't been this nervous since her PhD oral defence.

She cast a desperate eye around her immediate surroundings. Was she looking for an escape route or a distraction? She couldn't even tell, it felt as if her brain was detaching itself from her body and floating up into the ether, abandoning a sinking ship, perhaps. Just then Sophie noticed that about five metres away, standing on the other side of the entrance to the building, was a rumpled and worried-looking man-boy talking on the phone.

"Mum? No, listen, it's a small thing. I think... I hope," he added. Worry was creasing his brow and he was shifting from foot to foot, biting his thumb.

Sophie thought the two of them must look like anxious gargoyles guarding the building.

She watched as someone walked past him and said, "Morning Harry," patting him on the shoulder as they strode into the building. Harry nodded, but returned his attention to his phone call, gnawing on his lower lip before raising his hand to his mouth. "I know, I know." His voice dropped lower. "And don't worry, I won't lose my job, Mum. You don't have to worry about that."

To Sophie, his assurance didn't sound at all convincing and she found herself hoping that his mother believed him. As a sweet fruity smell wafted over to her, Sophie realised he was vaping and wondered if that helped calm the nerves. This Harry person, who was sucking away at the pipe like it was his source of oxygen, certainly seemed to think so. She made a mental note to look it up then checked the time. Her stomach fluttered nervously. Her appointment was in five minutes and it was time to go inside. Sophie took a deep breath, straightened her skirt, and walked through the doors toward the immaculate receptionist.

"Good morning," Sophie said in her best grown-up voice. "Dr Swanephol. I have a meeting with Josh Spencer." She was pleased a nervous tremor wasn't audible.

The receptionist's eyes flicked up to Sophie and then down again. "Take a seat," she murmured, her fingers flying over her keyboard.

"Right." Sophie nodded confidently.

A couch and two armchairs were placed amongst several oversized plants in an area directly opposite the reception desk. Sophie settled in one of the armchairs and picked up a magazine, but kept her eyes up so she could watch the people streaming in and out of the foyer. They all wore Business Suits; had Official-Looking Lanyards; were engaged in Important Business Talk; or conducting on-the-go Conference Calls as they strode past.

Things were a Go in the Land of Business.

Sophie noticed a watercooler directly to her right and suddenly became aware of how dry her mouth was. She stood to help herself to a cup of water, filled it a second time, and then a third, guzzling it back as if it could quell her nervousness. Then, she suddenly thought in a panic, what if I need to go to the toilet halfway through the meeting. That would hardly look professional. She'd seem as if she was so nervous she couldn't control her bladder, like a kid. She dropped the cup in the rubbish bin and returned to her seat, wondering if there was a toilet in the vicinity. She looked around for a sign, and then at the receptionist, who looked in the opposite direction. An unpleasant and ominous gurgle in Sophie's stomach threatened much more sinister toilet-based scenarios that she could be worrying about. It was now precisely ten thirty and Josh could arrive at any moment to take her to the meeting, but maybe she should risk it and go to the toilet. Surely it would be worse to have to excuse herself for a toilet emergency.

"Ahem."

Sophie looked up to see another person sitting in the waiting area. A man in his forties wearing an expensive-looking suit and a smile. Sophie wondered for a worried moment whether she had competition for this gig. The thought made her stomach clench even tighter with anxiety. Josh had made it seem like this was in the bag, but this meeting with *executives* had been a bit of a surprise. He'd assured her it was a formality, but then had tossed in at the end the casual but terrifying suggestion that she might have to do *some convincing.*

Sophie's palms were sweaty. Would they dry before she had to shake hands with anyone? Her stomach rolled and gurgled again. Oh god, who was she kidding, she couldn't do this on her own. Could she leave? Josh would understand, wouldn't he? She could get out of here and text him to say something urgent came up. Sophie cast panicked eyes around the room, looking for an escape. The man across from her, looking annoyingly relaxed with a newspaper on his knee, smiled again.

"So, what brings you here?" he said, either ignoring or completing misreading Sophie's demeanour, which was of someone who'd been taken hostage in a bank robbery.

"Sophie?" Josh appeared out of nowhere and Sophie jumped up so quickly she nearly tripped on her bag and catapulted herself into his arms.

Josh crooked his elbow and said, "Shall we?"

The gesture was not appropriate for a business meeting but Sophie's legs felt like jelly so she grasped his elbow and tried to act like a normal person.

LEO SCURRIED DOWN the driveway to his unit at the back of the large Mt Eden property. He kept low, so anyone standing in the kitchen of the main house who happened to be looking out the window wouldn't see him. That his parents were his landlords was humiliating enough, but the flat was also located on his parent's property. He didn't like that they could see him come and go, then casually comment on the nature of his schedule, with his father dropping in remarks about how different things were these days. But he still let his mother do his laundry and he still trundled over there for dinner when he had no food in the fridge—which occurred rather frequently. And while he had also recently become aware of the female-deflecting properties of the situation, what choice did he have?

When he opened the door Emmitt, the cat he'd recently adopted from the SPCA, was sitting on the bench glaring at him.

"Meow," Emmitt complained.

"Sorry, dude." Leo had crashed at Barrett's house last night—a gaming session had gotten away on them—and Emmitt had missed out on breakfast. "I brought you a treat to make up for it."

Leo held up the fresh chicken livers he'd picked up from the butcher and Emmitt started pacing the counter, purring with anticipation.

Leo was forgiven.

After dropping the meat into a dish, Leo pulled a packet of instant noodles from the cupboard. Meat from the butchers was not something Leo could afford for himself let alone his cat, but it wasn't Emmitt's fault and he couldn't let him suffer. And it was about time he sorted his finances out anyway because Barrett was becoming increasingly hostile. Last night's gaming session had been less of an invitation and more of a demand. When Barrett had lent him the money he'd good-naturedly assured Leo everything was sweet. But there was a time limit on that good nature, apparently. An incredibly brief one. He had a sneaking suspicion Barrett might soon start charging him interest.

Leo would have to pay Barrett back, but how? Paige and Sophie hadn't hired him for anything even though they had a corporate job. He'd catch up with them and ask again soon, Leo resolved, but in the meantime, it was probably worth having a look on TradeMe, or Seek. Just in case there was something he could do, some casual job he could fit in around his other duties.

The last thing he wanted was to give up working with S & S.


SOPHIE VIRTUALLY SKIPPED out of the building and took a moment, standing on the edge of the street to mentally *wooohooo!* She'd done it. She'd convinced the *boys upstairs* as Josh called them—and indeed the four executives seated around the table were indeed all men—to hire S & S to conduct psychometric tests for their organisation.

The meeting had been brief and two of the execs—Sophie had been too nervous to recall names—had excused themselves only twenty minutes in. But Josh had smiled at her the whole time and filled in blanks or added bits as needed. And one of the execs had been a kind-eyed older man who'd smiled at her in encouragement. Those two had made up for the intimidatingly large boardroom environment, and for the other two leaving early and spending the time they had been in the meeting flicking through their phones.

Sophie was beaming as she strode toward Britomart to get the bus back to the office—finding a park downtown was a gamble she hadn't been prepared to take on top of all those other jitters. When she got to the bus stop she pulled out her phone to call Paige but stopped when she saw the display.

She had a missed call from Roman.

He'd called an hour ago and he'd left a message. Feeling a little like this was a reward for having the guts to attend that meeting alone, Sophie listened to the message. Roman's lightly accented voice informed her that he thought maybe she could review any interviews they had on Terry's file. She could use her expertise to see if anything stood out or seemed amiss. Was she free to get together in a few days?

Sophie sucked back an excited gulp of air, saved the message, and texted him back to say *yes*.

AN HOUR LATER, Paige and Sophie settled in for lunch at Barilla Dumplings on Dominion Road. As they waited for chicken and celery dumplings and fried beans with spicy salt—termed *crack beans* because of how addictive they were—Paige thumbed through the contract Sophie had brought back from the meeting.

"Well done, Soph," Paige said. "We're in a trial period to start with, right?"

Sophie nodded. "If things go well, they might hire us for more further work, but as a start, Josh wants us to focus on the HR department, and do a sort of psychometric check-up."

"Not for new hires?"

"They don't have any vacancies at the moment and right now they're looking at a corporate restructure, so they want this testing to help with decisions."

"So, if we give them the kind of data they want, then they might extend our contract for the whole company?"

Sophie shrugged. "I guess. Or, maybe it would be more targeted, if they have an underperforming department, sales-wise, I guess? And they want, like, an audit for their staff?" Sophie shrugged again. "For now, we have to run tests on Josh's staff."

"But he doesn't want every test under the sun, surely."

"No. We chatted about that. He wants personality tests and general aptitude tests to make sure people are in the right jobs. We're going to do a check on people's understanding of their job descriptions as compared to their actual job descriptions, and then look at the personality fit. And then, once everyone has been tested, he wants an assessment of the departmental culture and any potential problems within the various teams."

"Like, personality clashes affecting productivity?"

"Right. And also how engaged his people are, overall."

Paige nodded. "Gotcha." She put the contract into her bag.

Sophie looked thoughtful. "Hey, we're not giving the execs ammunition with which to fire people, are we?"

"I don't know, but they aren't starving children, you know? These are fully functioning, educated adults, some of whom have probably been slacking and could do with a kick up the bum."

Sophie grinned. Paige's take on things was almost always insensitive-slash-blunt, but sometimes rather helpful.


Harry paused outside Josh Spencer's office, rapped twice on the door, then poked his head inside. "Hey. Is now a good time?"

Josh looked up. When he saw Harry he jumped up from his chair, hurried over to the door and peered out, scanning the corridor outside his office. "Yeah, come in."

Harry took a seat and cleared his throat. "Hey, um, you know Kate?"

"Just a sec. I need to get a couple of emails off," Josh said.

While Harry waited, shifting nervously in his chair.

Finally, Josh sat back and regarded Harry. "Good weekend?"

He was trying to seem cool and relaxed. Like a chill dude. But in reality, these meetings with Harry always made him a little nervous.

"Not bad. Hey, I was wondering... Do you know Kate? In payroll?"

Josh shrugged.

"Well, uh." Harry cleared his throat again. "The, uh, payroll report from last month..."

Josh held up his hand. "Harry, mate, talk to Michelle. She's your supervisor—I just run the show." He chuckled, as if he'd said something witty.

"But—"

"Hang on."

Josh checked once again that no one was loitering around outside his office, then closed the blinds.

# 7

With their temporary access cards in lanyards around their necks and a lot of nervous sighing from Sophie but self-important shuffling from Paige, the S & S Investigators were getting ready to start interviews. Josh had organised for them to each have a small meeting room on the third floor at their disposal for the duration of their contract.

"Okay, I'd better get next door," Sophie said with a nervous smile.

"Yep. See you at lunch." Paige nodded and took a seat at the desk. "Oh, hey. Someone came into S & S looking for you the other day. And it was the weirdest thing, Soph, she looked exactly like you."

Sophie paused at the door. "What?"

Paige shrugged. "She showed up, took your business card and left."

"And she looked exactly like me?" Sophie was rightly dubious. Facial recognition was not exactly Paige's strong suit.

Paige recounted the entirety of their brief interaction to Sophie.

"But who was she?"

"She'll call you, I'm sure of it," Paige said. There was a knock on the door. "We'll talk about it later," she added before calling out, "Come in."

Sophie eased past the robust young man who'd appeared in the doorway.

"Oh," he said. "I thought I had an appointment in here."

"You do." Sophie nodded at Paige. "But not with me."

He glanced into the room but then returned his gaze to Sophie.

"Ahem," Paige said loudly.

He frowned, peered into the room and said, "Oh, right. Didn't see you."

Sophie returned to her own meeting room a little dazed. She couldn't believe that someone who looked like her, named Hannah apparently, had walked in and out of their office without the normally pushy Paige gathering any useful information. She also couldn't believe it had ta' Paige *days* to remember to tell her. She sh

99

head. She wouldn't worry about it for now—Paige was probably mistaken.

JOSH CHECKED THE time, wondering if it would seem too keen if he went downstairs to check on Sophie.

He'd done his darnedest to get her sitting somewhere on the tenth floor—near his office and away from the small pushy one, who he could already tell might end up cramping his style—so that he would be more easily able to swing by and call on Sophie whenever he felt like it. But he'd had no luck. The office manager Denise had glared at him with suspicion when he'd asked about spaces on the tenth floor, and narrowed her eyes with irritation when he'd tried to fluff over the reason for it, so he'd dropped the matter. Denise was in charge of booking all the meeting rooms and the only one who knew which forms were needed for what and where to find them—you couldn't fart inside these office walls without having a request and approval form completed—so Denise was not someone you wanted to upset.

"And she looked exactly like me?" Sophie was rightly dubious. Facial recognition was not exactly Paige's strong suit.

Paige recounted the entirety of their brief interaction to Sophie.

"But who was she?"

"She'll call you, I'm sure of it," Paige said. There was a knock on the door. "We'll talk about it later," she added before calling out, "Come in."

Sophie eased past the robust young man who'd appeared in the doorway.

"Oh," he said. "I thought I had an appointment in here."

"You do." Sophie nodded at Paige. "But not with me."

He glanced into the room but then returned his gaze to Sophie.

"Ahem," Paige said loudly.

He frowned, peered into the room and said, "Oh, right. Didn't see you."

Sophie returned to her own meeting room a little dazed. She couldn't believe that someone who looked like her, named Hannah apparently, had walked in and out of their office without the normally pushy Paige gathering any useful information. She also couldn't believe it had taken Paige *days* to remember to tell her. She shook her head. She wouldn't worry about it for now—Paige was probably mistaken.

JOSH CHECKED THE time, wondering if it would seem too keen if he went downstairs to check on Sophie.

He'd done his darnedest to get her sitting somewhere on the tenth floor—near his office and away from the small pushy one, who he could already tell might end up cramping his style—so that he would be more easily able to swing by and call on Sophie whenever he felt like it. But he'd had no luck. The office manager Denise had glared at him with suspicion when he'd asked about spaces on the tenth floor, and narrowed her eyes with irritation when he'd tried to fluff over the reason for it, so he'd dropped the matter. Denise was in charge of booking all the meeting rooms and the only one who knew which forms were needed for what and where to find them—you couldn't fart inside these office walls without having a request and approval form completed—so Denise was not someone you wanted to upset.

SOPHIE FLICKED HER eyes from the HR file on the desk in front of her back to McKenna Bryston's face. According to the file, she was in her late twenties and had only been employed for three months, but already had a formal warning on record. For what, Sophie did not know. Even though they'd signed a confidentiality agreement they did not have a full access pass to HR files.

McKenna leaned forward and continued talking about how she had single-handedly revolutionised the way they processed absence requests. Sophie was almost certain this wasn't true. She'd realised McKenna had narcissistic tendencies almost immediately, but now, after spending twenty minutes with her, she was beginning to believe she might have a diagnosable case of narcissistic personality disorder sitting in front of her. Sophie wondered whether this nugget of information was on the redacted section of the file. Or perhaps this is the very thing they wanted to uncover, Sophie mused. She should have another conversation with Josh about exactly what they wanted in the individual files they were creating for each employee. When she made a note of this McKenna's eyes lit up, believing she'd said something particularly important. Enthused and validated, she carried on with gusto. Sophie suppressed a sigh. Sophie's only utterance so far had been to check she had the right person in front of her and confirm her role in the organisation. From then it had been a constant stream of grandiose and self-congratulatory speechifying. It was like hanging out with Victoria, Sophie thought, but at least she was getting paid to listen to this.

"Right," Sophie said the moment McKenna paused to take a breath. "Let's get you started on this questionnaire, shall we?" Sophie coaxed her dormant laptop into life and started the programme. They were using their own personal laptops for this but pretending they were business laptops so they seemed more professional. This meant Sophie had spent several hours yesterday removing all her shortcuts to various non-professional looking things and photos on her desktop. She'd even changed the screensaver so it had their S & S logo, but she suspected Paige had not done the same, which meant that at least some of the employees were likely to see Paige's desktop background, which was a photo of herself, Paige and Tim during a New Year's Eve celebration.

Sophie turned the laptop around so that McKenna had access to the keyboard and stood up. "I'll stay in the room, but I'll be over there, so call out if you have any questions. I won't be able to help you decide on an answer, of course, but just in case anything goes wrong or there is an issue with the instructions, for example."

McKenna nodded, her eyes gleaming with excitement at the prospect of talking about herself, albeit to an inanimate object, for a little bit longer.


SHARON CROSS, THE office administrator, was a little shorter and a touch wider than average, and had shoulder-length brown hair that was attempting to be a 'Rachel' cut. Like the majority of women who asked hairdressers for this nineties hairstyle, she had not been transformed into Jennifer Aniston as a result, and had remained an ordinary woman who now had a haircut with inexplicably different lengths. But for Sharon, at least, the overall look had been improved by the addition of highlights framing her face.

Sharon was currently in the interview room with Paige, and had now been sitting in silence for nearly a minute while Paige eyeballed her.

She shifted in her seat. "Cross is my name, but it's not my game," she said with a nervous laugh.

Paige squinted at her. "Huh?"

"Oh, it's just a ditty I came up with. My surname is Cross but I'm almost never in a bad mood," she added with a nervous smile.

Sharon had sailed into the interview room entirely confident in the security of her job, but now uncertainty was picking at her. Why was this young woman glaring at her? When asked to give an overview of her role, Sharon had tried to explain, without sounding full of herself, that she was the glue that held this department together. She knew everybody really well; was responsible for team morale; and she was always the first person people came to when they needed something, or to talk.

Sharon was, in Sharon's opinion, the heart of the operation. In reality, Sharon was the office gossip, and people came to her when they were bored and needed something juicy to get them through the afternoon.

Although she'd started as a relatively diligent employee, Sharon's need for chit-chat was far greater than any sense of work ethic or desire to reduce the size of her To-Do list, and so she spent a great deal of time wandering around the office looking for conversation. All it took was the slightest indication of interest and she would settle in for a good old chinwag. Almost entirely one-sided, of course. And once Sharon got comfortable, one was stuck with her for at least fifteen minutes, which might not sound like a long time, but her stories were meandering and full of unnecessary detail as well as cringe-worthy sentiments, and it usually became an agonising wait for her to finish. The trouble was, she often delivered something good at the end, and the next time she sidled up one's memory would latch onto this, forgetting how painful the previous fifteen minutes had been. Thirty seconds in and they'd remember, but by then it was too late.

Paige tapped her pen against the desk and Sharon shifted in her chair again. She was beginning to worry that her job might be at stake.

Paige suddenly leaned forward "Anything you want to tell me?"

Sharon, for the first time in her life unsure of what to say, merely blinked and shook her head.

"Okay. You can do the questionnaire now." Paige swung the laptop around and nodded at Sharon.

"What happens with the results of this survey? Do my answers get scored or something?"

"The personality part gets scored, but it's not the kind of score where a higher number is better. The aim is to see how different personality types fit into the organisational, or team, culture."

Sharon felt a little better. If she was sure of one thing it was that her personality fit perfectly within the team. She turned her attention to the questions in front of her.

"Oh, but what is this about how I spend my day?"

"As I said at the start, there are two parts to this."

Sharon blinked, trying to think back to what Paige had said earlier but she had absolutely no recollection. Instead of listening, she'd been trying to think about the best example she could give about how everyone needed her and came to her for advice.

"First, you tell us what your job involves—in your words—as well as what you do in a typical day. Your normal tasks. And *then* it's the personality test."

Sharon cast one more glance at Paige before, with a little flutter of worry, turning her attention to the laptop. She didn't know that her role in the team was something that could be itemised like this. Not in a way that would do it justice, and certainly not into these brief intervals, which were, ironically, fifteen minutes each.

At a few minutes past two o'clock, Sophie and Paige were seated in one of the meeting rooms on the tenth floor, wondering how this had happened. Sophie risked a wide-eyed glance at Paige. Paige returned the glance with an eye roll.

How had they ended up in the two-hour weekly HR meeting? This was one of the reasons they'd escaped academia—the endless and pointless meetings in which you could count on circular discussions, ego-stroking, pontificating and agenda-pushing. As it turned out, meetings in the corporate environment were not so different—it seemed only jargon that separated the two. And they weren't even being paid for this extra meeting because they'd agreed on a set fee to conduct their interviews and write up a report.

"Thanks for that update, Pearl," Josh said, casting a warm smile around the table. "Now, Jim, what about the FTE situation?"

"Ah yes," a small man with greyish skin said. He licked his surprisingly pink lips and started reading something from the papers in front of him. For every few words he uttered, he paused to cough twice. It was a dry cough that didn't appear to achieve anything except be extremely irritating. After a minute Sophie's phone, sitting on her lap on vibrate, buzzed. It was a text from Paige.

*OMG I am going to murder this man.*

...

*For the love of God, someone give him a lozenge.*

Sophie's hand shot to her mouth to cover up her smile. She could feel Paige's eyes burning into hers, but if she looked at her, she would erupt into giggles. For sure. Instead, she cast her eyes across to Jim. His report had at least five sheets of paper stapled together.

This was excruciating.

Why were they here?

Sophie caught Josh's eye. He winked and smiled.

Oh, Sophie thought, that's why.

AT TEN PAST five Paige and Sophie left the already throbbing downtown area to have a quick Friday night drink at *Love Bucket* on K' Road.

K' Road, known for its grungy clubs and all-night partying, was still relatively serene at this early hour and Sophie planned on being long gone by the time the first wave of party people—those pre-loading at cheap BYO restaurants—started filling the streets.

They entered the bar and walked past the dark, corner booths—good for a date, Sophie found herself thinking as an image of Roman popped into her head—and past the smattering of tables in the middle, to sit at the back, right under the window facing out to Myers Park. The air was heavy, muggy with the potential of rain, but there was a patch of optimistic blue sky persevering in the north and this was the direction they faced.

The waitress came over and they ordered a glass of wine each. Paige went for an expensive

Shiraz, whereas Sophie chose the house red because it was on special for Happy Hour.

"Hey, did you know that everyone has like, a set amount of words that they need to use in a day," Paige said. "If you don't use them up, you have verbal diarrhoea with the next person you see. But if you do use all your words in a day, then you find it hard to make conversation."

Sophie nodded. Not only had she heard that theory before, she herself had experienced it. During her PhD on those blissful days she worked at home, she would—completely out of character—pounce on her flatmates when they came home from work, craving conversation. Tonight however, it was the opposite. Her words were most definitely nearly used up. In these times she was glad to have flatmates like Myra, who could sit in silence all evening, and Victoria, who was happy to carry on an entire conversation completely on her own.

The waitress came over and deposited their wine and some sunflower seeds for them to nibble on.

"Great," Sophie said dully, gazing at her phone. "Josh friend requested me."

"I wonder if I have a request too," Paige said drily.

"Should I ignore it? If I accept it now, I feel like he'll start messaging me tonight. He's out at drinks right now." Sophie rolled her eyes. "He made a point of telling me earlier."

"Definitely wait, then." Paige checked her own phone. "Hey, Leo's keen to hang out. Shall I tell him to come join us?"

"Sure. But I'm going after this wine, okay?" It had been a long week and Sophie was knackered.

Paige nodded. "Tim said dinner would be ready at seven o'clock, so I can hang with Leo for a bit."

Sophie suppressed a surge of jealousy at Paige's seeming domestic bliss, and shoved a few sunflower seeds into her mouth. But maybe domestic bliss was just around the corner for her too.

They sipped their wine as they compared notes about their interviews, agreeing that the corporate environment might be as odd as the academic one.

"I think it's just that in general, people are kind of weird," Sophie mused, "and we all pretend we aren't, but the moment you start asking questions, trying to measure us, human beings, it becomes obvious."

Paige chuckled. Her phone, still sitting on the table, beeped. "Leo's nearly here." Paige typed out a quick response then saw that she had a message from Tim. A YouTube clip. Expecting to see a cat-fail video, or similar, she pressed play and instead saw a montage of babies and toddlers covered in flour, chocolate, paint, makeup... and every other substance under the sun that toddlers could adorably get themselves covered in while their parents were distracted. It was pretty cute, Paige had to admit, but she thought that the frequency with which Tim was showing her these cute-kid videos might be increasing.

"Ladies!" Leo bellowed. "I'll get myself a beer and join you," he shouted from across the bar, his voice piercing the thrum of intense but quiet conversation. Sometimes Leo seemed to know just the right thing to say but other times he could be completely clueless.

"He's looking pretty trim, aye?" Sophie said, eyeing him.

Paige turned to regard Leo as he approached. "Have you lost weight?" she said when Leo was in earshot.

Leo reddened. "I guess," he said, shuffling his feet. Leo was, in fact, on somewhat of a diet. The unexpected but welcome arrival of Paige and Sophie in his life had spurred him into new behaviours. He'd cut back on the regularity in which he chowed down entire packets of chips and was trying to eat better across the board. This was difficult when one was on a limited budget, but he'd managed to switch from white bread to boiled or grilled potatoes as his main carbohydrate, he'd cut back on sugar, and he'd stopped drinking coke completely. The weight had fallen off with these seemingly small, but rather important dietary changes, and after an initial few days of feeling like crap as his body withdrew from coca cola, he was now feeling much better than he could ever remember.

Sophie drained her glass. "Hey Leo, it's nice to see you, but I'm heading off now," she said with an apologetic smile.

"No worries. I'll come by the office soon for a catch-up."

Sophie left money for her wine with Paige and waved goodbye.

"I need a job," Leo said, taking Sophie's seat.

"You know we've got a corporate gig, right?"

"Yeah. There's nothing else?"

Paige studied Leo's forlorn expression and felt sorry enough him to give the matter some serious thought. Out of nowhere, an image of her mother, sweaty and red as she yanked weeds out of her garden, popped into her head.

"How much are you willing to endure?" Paige asked.

WHEN SOPHIE GOT home Victoria was taking an after-work shower, which meant one of two things: either she was going out and she'd float out of the bathroom in a cloud of body lotions and wearing an ear to ear grin; or she'd had a terrible day and would slouch into the living room in her bathrobe and infect everyone within a one-kilometre radius with her bad mood.

"What's the situation in there?" Sophie asked Myra, sitting on the couch in the living room with a textbook on her lap and a cup of tea balanced on the arm rest.

Myra shook her head, eyes wide. "Don't know. She's been in there for ages."

Sophie placed her six-pack of KFC chicken wings on the table, trying not to look or feel guilty. Her bus stop was literally right outside the Pt Chev

KFC and it seemed as if they pumped the smell out onto the street to entice customers inside. It was very effective, and one pack of chicken wings was rather restrained, she thought. "How's the studying going?" she asked as she shrugged off her coat. Before Myra could answer, the lock to the bathroom clicked. Sophie and Myra tensed in anticipation.

"Oooh, Sophie! Great. You can help me decide what to wear!" Victoria beamed. "Well, it's only between two dresses. But it's still a big choice," she added, her eyes wide and serious. "And then there's the shoes… and hair up or down… and the style of makeup." Victoria did a twirl and scampered to her room.

That's right, Sophie recalled, tonight was the company ball Victoria had been going on about for the last week. She'd been graciously invited to join someone in her department's table—based on the timing, it seemed to Sophie that Victoria was filling an unexpected vacancy—and she'd been in seventh heaven since then, discussing and planning everything to do with that night down to a shocking level of detail. From what Sophie could tell, Victoria had been plucked, waxed, highlighted, bronzed, massaged, manicured *and* pedicured in preparation for tonight.

An excited thump came from Victoria's room.

Sophie hoped she would have a good time, and that these "work friends" she had started talking about didn't exclude her in any obvious or mean way. For all her insufferableness, Victoria wasn't a bad person, and she seemed so happy to be invited to something it made Sophie's heart ping. As she reached for her chicken wings she resolved to be a better friend—or at least *something* of a friend to her.

MEANWHILE, AFTER LEAVING Paige, Leo had made the mistake of popping in to see Barrett, who was now eying Leo with what was unmistakeably hostility. This was getting ridiculous. Barrett was acting like if Leo didn't pay back his money immediately, he would be bankrupted and cast out onto the street, and this was far from true. Leo had met Barrett's mother and she would do anything for Barrett. She was basically his servant.

"Can't you give me a break? You don't need the money."

"Listen, I've had second thoughts. Money gets between friends. I shouldn't have lent it to you."

"Okay fine. I've been offered a gardening job. I'll take it and pay you back as soon as I get paid. Is that good enough?"

"Gardening?"

"Shut up. I'll see you later."

As Leo walked away he pulled his phone out and brought up Paige's mother's number. Unease crept into his shoulders as he made the call. Paige's mother, Alice Garnet, was one of his pet napping 'victims'. Her cat, the extremely chilled out TomTom, had been the very first pet he'd nabbed but he didn't know whether Alice was aware of this or not. It was entirely possible that Paige had forgotten all about it. Or maybe Alice was like one of those trusting business owners who gave criminals a second chance? Based on what Paige had said about her mother, it seemed unlikely. No, Leo thought, she probably didn't know. In which case, if he did start working for Alice, should he confess? Get it out in the open straight away and explain?

He sighed. He'd figure it out later if he got this job. The idea of him gardening was kind of ridiculous. But what else could he do?

# 8

The next morning Paige was driving down New North Road past the office when she spotted Hazel at the entrance to the building, about to ascend the stairs.

Paige made the spontaneous decision to pull over, earning a couple of indignant beeps from the flow of cars. She parked in a ten-minute spot, then hurried over to the entrance. When she got to the top of the stairs, Hazel was locking her office door.

"Hazel?"

She turned, gripping a satchel-type bag under her arm and holding her keys in one hand with a thermos in the other. "Paige." Hazel smiled, her eyes bright and warm. "Just the person. I was going to see if we could catch up next week? Maybe Wednesday or Thursday? To talk about that possible job."

Paige stared at Hazel. She seemed totally fine. Alert, energetic, nothing like the woman who had nearly fainted; nor the woman who'd been really weird a few days before that.

"Um, okay. I have a few minutes now, if you like."

Paige was on her way to another day of interviews and in truth, they were getting a little boring. At first it had been a thrill, getting access to people's files, but she had since discovered that listening to people talk about their job and then sitting quietly while they did the online portion of the tests could be very, very dull. She wanted to do a good job, of course, she was all too aware of how important this kind of work was as an income stream, but as her boredom grew, she was increasingly finding herself looking for other things to keep her interested. Like the possible case Hazel had mentioned.

"Rather a full day, I'm afraid," Hazel said. "My afternoon lesson cancelled so I'm going to take this opportunity to run a few long overdue errands. I only popped in to pick up some papers and my lunch," she explained, holding up her thermos. "How's that psychometric testing job going? Do you have capacity for more work?"

"It's not the most exciting thing I've ever done and yes, we can make space for you."

"Good. Okay, I'll talk to you next week, if not before."

Paige watched Hazel go, and after a moment shrugged to herself and decided she would be optimistic about this Hazel situation.

JOSH APPEARED IN the doorway of Sophie's meeting room and strolled over to lean against the edge of the table. "I run a pretty tight ship, you know," he said.

They'd been doing interviews for over a week now and Sophie had met with a number of his direct reports. What they had to say about the *SS Josh* suggested this was not in fact true. He seemed much more interested in playing with the boys upstairs, Sophie had noticed, practically panting whenever he had a meeting with them. He'd also spent rather a lot of time down here, hovering around as if checking on their progress. Sophie, while grateful for the job and for having Josh on her side, was getting a bit tired of having to laugh at his jokes. Maybe she should stop. It was encouraging him, after all. But how does one not laugh when someone thinks they've made a joke and are staring at you, eyes bright and wide as they nodded, expecting you to laugh too? What kind of sociopath could just sit there with a neutral expression in the face of that? Paige could, Sophie thought immediately. Then she felt bad. Paige wasn't a sociopath, not by a long shot. She was just lucky enough to be unbothered by some of the more taxing social graces Sophie and the rest of the world were burdened by.

"Did you hear me, Soph?"

Josh was calling her *Soph*, now?

"Yes, sorry. I've only really started the interviews, it will take a while before we know what is what. I've got a lot of people to get through." Sophie hoped Josh might take the hint.

"Oh." Josh was crestfallen. "Hey, do you want to grab coffee? Could, uh…" he snapped his fingers, "the other one… um…" Josh waved his hand and frowned as he tried to recall Paige's name. "Could she cover for you? I want to try the new coffee place around the corner but I don't want to go alone." Josh pouted.

Sophie wondered whether pouting was a technique that had ever worked for Josh. It must have at least once before, and she knew from experimental studies with pigeons it could take many, many instances of displaying a behaviour with no reward before it was extinguished.

"Sorry, we both have interviews. And I couldn't leave work like that." Sophie smiled. "It wouldn't suggest a very good work ethic, would it?"

"No, of course. Well, an after-work drink one night then." Josh perked up when he realised this was a much better prospect.

"Oh, erm. Sure. Not this week, though, things on every night, you know. But another time, maybe."

"Oh course, yeah, now that I think about it, I've got a full week too, but next week, for sure. Great." Josh jumped up. "Right... Get back to it minion." He mimed cracking a whip and attempted a light-hearted chuckle but the whole bit fell horribly flat and then lingered like a bad smell.

"Oh, ha-ha," Sophie said, taking pity on him and forcing a smile.

The corner of Josh's mouth turned down as he left the room. He'd bungled that one but, he thought, there'd be time to make up for it. He'd have a whole evening with her next week to impress. He'd watched *The Nice Guys* last night, and with practice, he fancied he'd be able to finally master that goofy but still manly thing Ryan Gosling had working for him.

Sophie's two o'clock appointment was the twitchy young man she'd seen waiting outside the building that day she'd had the meeting with the executives. His name was Harry and he shuffled into Sophie's interview room with the same nervous expression he'd been wearing that first day. She eyed him. Early twenties, scrawny and taller than average. His hair needed a wash and he had a grey tinge to his skin that suggested a lack of fruit and vegetables. Or worse.

"Harry," Sophie stated, rather than asked. His HR file was in front of her, so his position, supervisor, and even pay grade were all right there. What the file didn't tell her was the reason for his obvious distress.

Sophie started the interview as she normally would, asking him for a description of his role in general, and for a more detailed breakdown of how he spent his day. These two questions had so far proved to be extremely informative. The extent of the mismatch between official job descriptions and what employees thought their job entailed was rather incredible, but Sophie saw the main role of the questions more as a way to warm up the individual for the excel spreadsheet which required them to document how they spent their workday in fifteen-minute increments. It was an awful task to ask of a human being and one that simply begged people to be untruthful. But it was standard practice.

"Here you are. If you could fill this out for today, so far. Your morning."

"Okay," Harry mumbled. All he'd done this morning was sit on the toilet for two separate and equally miserable and unproductive twenty-minute periods—there was no way he was writing that down—and carried on worrying about the information he'd stumbled upon. But he knew what a normal day looked like, so he wrote that down.

Once he'd finished Sophie turned the laptop back to face her. "Oh, you handle the KiwiSaver stuff," she said with a smile. "I got myself a KiwiSaver account in undergrad. It seemed like such a commitment at the time, but now, I can see the benefit of a having a savings plan. You can use your savings to buy your first home; you can pull it out if you get really sick or something; and of course, it will be nice to have that nest egg for when I'm old and sick of working." Sophie gave Harry a friendly smile, but Harry had turned ashen. "Are you okay, Harry? You don't look—"

"I feel sick." Harry stood abruptly, holding his stomach. "Can we... uh... I have to go."

Harry turned and bolted.

The next day Sophie had three interviews booked, but the first didn't start until ten thirty, which meant she had time to follow up with Harry. At the very least she had to reschedule the rest of his interview and run him through the test. But more than that, she was worried about him. He did not seem to be in a good state at all. Was it something to do with work, or his personal life? Sophie looked up his desk location. Then, making sure her bag was tucked away out of sight in the drawer and she had her phone, she went off in search of Harry.

HARRY WAS SITTING in a toilet stall, not achieving much of anything.

He'd come in here to get away from his desk—from that spreadsheet—but as soon as he'd swung open the door and been confronted with the stale bathroom air and fluorescent lights, he'd been reminded of the dull pressure in his abdomen. But it was a pressure with no urgency to it, Harry was discovering once again. He adjusted himself on the seat and wondered how long this was going to take. There was a draft in here—which was odd because as far as he knew, there was no source of outside air in the building—and the exposed skin of his buttocks was getting cold. He did not have enough body fat to stand this much longer, but he had to at least try. This was day three in the toilet stalemate and how long could one person go without... going? He tried to make himself relax but his mind would not stop racing, and it seemed to be giving his intestines instructions to close up shop. A small, involuntary sound of desperation escaped Harry.

"You alright in there, mate?" someone asked.

Harry didn't recognise the voice. "Yeah," he called back through the door, hoping they would go away, but no, the next thing he heard was the sound of another toilet stall opening and closing. He stood up and gave the unused toilet a flush. There was no way it was happening now.

Upon exiting the men's bathroom, he found himself face to face with Sophie.

"Oh, just the man I was looking for," she said, attempting cheeriness. "How are you feeling?"

Harry gave a shaky so-so gesture with his hand.

"Oh, that's a shame. But we really have to do that interview at some point, and I'm free now? If you're feeling up to it, that is," Sophie added.

"Um," he cleared his throat, "okay, sure."

"Great. Follow me."


AT A LITTLE before two o'clock, Sharon Cross strolled into the tearoom.

Paige was inside, scrolling through Instagram as she waited for her coffee to brew. Sharon thought at first that the room was empty and was disappointed—a rather strong craving for a cup of tea and a bit of a chitchat was what had propelled her here in the first place—until a motion next to the coffee machine drew her eyes over there and alerted her to the presence of another person. Sharon wasn't sure who it was, but it didn't even matter.

"Coo-eee," she trilled happily.

Paige cocked her head backward, the minimum angle needed to get the approximation of attention or acknowledgement and said, "Hi," then returned to her phone.

"You must have a touch of three-thirty-itis, like me," Sharon said with a chuckle.

"It's only two o'clock," Paige said without turning.

"Oh yes. Well... After lunch slump, then," Sharon persisted.

Paige nodded then shrugged her shoulders. Sharon forced herself into Paige's line of sight, and only then recognized her.

"Oh." The worried feeling Sharon had when she left her session with Paige came flooding back. "Um." She felt she needed to make a better impression somehow, but Paige was still staring at her phone.

"Is that a funny video?" Sharon said brightly, moving closer so that she could look over Paige's shoulder.

Paige remained where she was and took a controlled breath. "Sharon. Can I ask you something?"

"Of course."

"You have sensation in your boobs, right?"

"W-what?" Sharon reddened.

"You know, nerve endings, that send messages from your mammary glands to your brain to tell you about the sensation of touch?"

"Um... of course I do, yes."

"So you can feel that they, your boobs, are currently pressing up against my shoulder?"

"What, oh, goodness, I'm sorry." The colour in Sharon's face deepened.

"Sharon?"

"Yes?"

"They're still there."

"Goodness." Sharon finally moved away from Paige, the squishy heat subsiding.

"Thanks," Paige said cheerfully, taking her coffee and leaving the room.

Sharon watched her go, wondering what to make of her, and whether she should ignore or attend to this sinking feeling that she'd made the situation even worse.

ROMAN SLID HIS phone into his pocket and stood up. He and Sophie had arranged to meet next week to discuss Terry Garnet's case, and while Roman had a rather full caseload, he would make time for this. And no time like the present. It was too important to ignore.

He left his desk and headed down to the basement where the old case files were kept. He couldn't show up to their meeting empty-handed. Sophie had seemed rather impressed by what he'd worked out using the coast guard reports, and he'd rather like to impress her even further.

"Hey, Pete," he greeted the officer manning the desk. "How are things? How's your son doing down in Otago?"

Peter beamed. He could talk forever and a day about his eldest son, currently in his second year of a business degree at Otago University. Roman listened for five minutes as Pete described the intricate details of his son's life. Pete finally ran out of steam and said, "So what can I do for you Roman? What file are you after? Digging up some skeletons, aye?" he winked.

"Yeah, something like that." Roman pushed the piece of paper on which he'd written the reference number toward Pete who picked it up and ambled down one of the many rows of boxes of archived files.

Some of it was computerised, but there were always physical evidence and often looking at photograph wasn't enough. Sometimes you needed to sit with the information, the scrap of evidence, and hold it in your hands, to properly see things other people might have missed. The eye had the tendency to skim over things on screen, and Roman needed to make sure he wasn't missing anything. If he was going to do this—take a closer look at the details surrounding Terry Garnet's death—then he had to do it properly.

As Roman waited for Pete, rustling happily in the back of the room, he wondered what Sophie was doing right now. He could call her and let her know what he was up to, he mused. It seemed like a paper-thin excuse to talk to her, but so what? It was just a phone call. No, it wasn't that simple, Roman knew, but what if it could be?

"Roman. Roman? The files?"

Brought back to reality with a thump, Roman took the files with an apologetic smile. "Head in the clouds." He smiled. "Cheers."

AS SOON AS Paige finished her last interview she, knowing Sophie had already gone home, made her way back to the S & S office. Halfway through the day she'd realised she'd left her phone charger there and Tim, rather inconveniently, had an iPhone, which meant his charger was incompatible with her Samsung.

As Paige climbed the stairs she saw there was a light on in Hazel's office so she went over to 2A. Perhaps now was a good time to talk about that potential case. After a quick rap she opened the door.

"Oh... hello... there." Hazel was startled to the point of looking confused. She shook her head. "How is the... the..."

"The psychometric testing?"

"Yes." Hazel looked relieved. "Paige. How is the testing going?"

"Fine." Paige spoke slowly as she studied Hazel's face. She was experiencing the trippy sensation of déjà vu, except it wasn't a neural trick. They'd had this actual conversation, just this morning.

"What are you doing here?" Paige asked.

Hazel frowned, looking even more confused. "What do you mean?"

"Didn't your afternoon lessons get cancelled?"

Hazel looked down to the notepad in front of her. "No... they didn't show up."

"Hazel... um... you told me this morning a lesson had been cancelled."

"This morning?"

A sick feeling swirled through Paige's stomach.

"Oh, yes. Sorry. Too many things on my mind."

"Hazel... are you okay?"

"I'm fine. Sorry, but I have to make a phone call. Do you mind?" She gestured at the door.

Paige shook her head. "See you later," she said in a small voice.

Several hours later, at home and snuggled on the couch with Tim, Paige shut her laptop with a sigh. Hazel was definitely showing signs of neurocognitive decline. She was in her seventies so some cognitive difficulties were normal, sure, but Paige thought something was wrong with Hazel, and she didn't feel good about this. Not at *all*.

# 9

There was another plate of biscuits waiting for Sophie when she arrived at her interview room, the second lot this week. Courtesy of Sharon, the note said, for both her and Paige. Paige was the one who had interviewed her, but yesterday Sharon had popped her head into Sophie's office when Paige was busy and rather inexplicably proceeded to talk for nearly half an hour about what a diligent employee she was. And now this. Did Sharon stay up all night, every night, baking? Was the whole HR department pre-diabetic by now? Maybe she and Paige should be testing blood-sugar levels instead of personality.

Sophie took one cookie to have with her coffee and transferred the rest to Paige's room, then returned to her laptop to check Harry's availability for a follow-up meeting this morning. She and Paige had been set up with full calendar access, so

Sophie could see this by selecting his name from the list. With nothing in Harry's calendar except the vague notation of 'appointment' at three o'clock, Sophie went ahead and scheduled a follow-up for ten a.m., today, in a little under an hour. Yesterday, she'd managed to get him to finish the interview and do the psychometric test, but the whole time he'd been uncomfortable to the point of near panic. There were signs of paranoia, considerable stress, and hints of worrying lifestyle choices. Sophie wasn't sure if this was within her job description, to investigate and report on employees who might be in a bad way, but she couldn't let it go. She had to at least ask him if he was okay. What if his mum was counting on him for his income or something? What if something was wrong, and Sophie was the only one who'd noticed, and did nothing?

Ten o'clock came and went with no sign of Harry. Sophie wasn't altogether surprised—he hadn't accepted her meeting request.

At eleven thirty, after a follow-up interview with McKenna the narcissist who'd insisted on another session because she felt she hadn't explained herself properly the first time—she of course had, far too thoroughly, but Sophie knew

McKenna had been so thrilled to sit in a room and talk to a captive audience about how fabulous she was she couldn't resist an opportunity to do it again—Sophie went to find Harry.

On the eighth floor, Harry wasn't at his desk. But Sophie only had to ask a couple of people before she found someone who knew where Harry was. Denise, the all-knowing and omnipotent office manager, had shuffled papers on her desk as she answered Sophie's question. "He went home sick," she said. "He made it to work but went home almost straight away. He looked terrible. We can't have him infecting the rest of us." Denise nodded resolutely. "Even though we're down two payroll clerks at the moment."

Sophie became aware of someone to her left staring at her. She turned her head only slightly, so that her peripheral vision could catch out who it was without them realising. A blonde woman wearing a beautiful charcoal suit stood in the door of a glass-walled office at the end of the corridor, gazing in their direction. She was most definitely listening to this conversation, and rather intently, it seemed. Just as Sophie turned her head further, Josh appeared and went over to talk to her.

Together, they went into her office and shut the door.

Sophie thought there was something overly familiar about the way they were with each other. If she had to put money on it, she would say they used to date. Or they'd at least slept together. There were tell-tale signals, like the small amount of distance between the woman and Josh as he moved past into her office. There wasn't the usual office co-worker sized bubble of personal space.

"Sophie? Hello? What do you need him for?" Denise was asking Sophie.

"Oh, a follow-up. He didn't seem very well. Do you think he's okay?"

Denise glared at her. "He's sick, isn't he?"

"Yes, but—"

"How would I know? I'm not a doctor."

"Right, of course."

Denise marched away.

Sophie returned to the third floor lost in thought. Going home sick was a relatively normal thing to do, but in conjunction with the way he'd acted yesterday, she couldn't help but feel uneasy.

ALICE GARNET SURVEYED her garden with a notepad in hand, intending to make a list of tasks she would give this Leo person her daughter had organised to help her, but found herself instead wondering what she would do with herself this evening. She often tried to remember how she and Terry had spent the time, but these memories eluded her. They can't have sat in here, doing nothing. No, they were probably out at some event, or having friends around. They had been quite social, the two of them. But things had changed after Terry had died. Perhaps Alice hadn't done enough to keep up with their friends. No matter she thought, squaring her shoulders, tonight she would read her book—it was getting rather good—and have a bath.

"Excuse me? Mrs Garnet? I'm Leo. I'm, uh, here."

Alice turned to see Leo standing at the edge of her garden. She took in his jeans, jandals and t-shirt, and couldn't decide whether she was irritated that he was so casually dressed, or because he wasn't *more* casually dressed, wearing overalls or something else suitable for gardening. This was a *favour* she was doing for her daughter. Another one. And it seemed as if this young man wasn't taking it seriously. Either that or he didn't have a clue. It was the latter, of course, but Alice did not yet know Leo well enough to realise this.

ALL LEO'S PREVIOUS notions of admitting to being TomTom's abductor had gone out the window. He couldn't stop staring at Alice. She reminded him so much of Paige. Much older, obviously, but she somehow didn't look as old as you'd expect. Did she have Paige when she was really, really young? Leo found himself wondering whether she had a husband. There was no sign of one, and wouldn't he be the one helping her in the garden, lugging bags of soil and yanking out weeds, if he existed? Leo then remembered that Paige's father had passed away a few years ago. Paige's mother, from what Leo could tell, did not seem to have remarried.

"Are you listening to me?" Alice was gesturing at the garden.

"Sorry, uh, not really," Leo admitted. "I was wondering how it was possible for you to have a daughter as old as Paige," he said truthfully.

"Oh, well." Alice reddened, touching her hand to her hair. "Thank you."

Leo shrugged. "It's true."

Alice tilted her head as her expression relaxed and something close to a smile crept on her face. "Were you planning on working in those clothes? They'll get dirty. Do you want something from my late husband's closet? I have a few singlets and things still, I think. You're rather bigger than he was," Alice patted her hair again, "but they'll do."

"Thanks," Leo said, looking down at his clothes and then at the mud in the garden, only now realising what working as a gardener might actually involve. This was a far cry from sitting in his armchair and tapping away on a keyboard. Leo turned his attention to watch Alice move gracefully into the house. She had to be in her fifties, but Leo didn't do the precise math because he found he didn't want to know.

SOPHIE STARED AT her phone. All thoughts and worries about Harry had disappeared.

Not only was she supposed to be meeting Roman in a little over an hour at five o'clock, she'd just received a text from the mysterious Hannah. Paige wasn't the most reliable witness, but she'd insisted Hannah was the spitting image of Sophie, and now Sophie was curious.

Hannah wanted to meet in Ponsonby, like, right now. It was important, her text said. With a nervous swirl in her stomach, Sophie saved Hannah as a new contact and sent her a message agreeing to meet. It bugged her, that she was so readily jumping to follow instructions from this person, but she found she couldn't ignore it.

When Sophie walked past Paige's door en route to the exit, it was closed. She sent her a quick text to let her know she'd gone for the day and headed for the stairs so she wouldn't bump into Josh as she made her escape. She'd already told him she was busy tonight, managing to put off the after-work drinks he'd been going on about once more, but he was rather persistent. At some point in the near future, Sophie knew, she would have to go for a drink with Josh. She'd just have to make sure Paige was there too, to act as a buffer.

Outside, she headed toward Britomart to find a bus that would take her to Ponsonby. At the bus stop she texted Roman, asking to change the location of their catch-up to Gypsy Tearoom in the nearby and less boisterous suburb of Grey Lynn. Or West Lynn, if you wanted to get technical. This way she'd be able to escape Ponsonby before the after-work drinks crowd appeared, and still have enough time to make her appointment with Roman. She'd been looking forward to seeing Roman all week, and she wouldn't be delaying it for this Hannah person. No matter who or what she looked like.

Sophie took a seat in the corner of Revelry on Ponsonby Road and waited. In a way, she was glad to have this distracting appointment before seeing Roman, it would mean she wouldn't have a chance to get all sweaty-nervous before she saw him.

Hannah walked in.

"Oh my god," Sophie said.

Paige hadn't been wrong, or exaggerating. Hannah looked *a lot* like her.

Hannah sat down across from Sophie, giving her a surreptitious once over as she did, and crossed her legs. She used her manicured, plum-coloured nails to adjust her long, artfully waved hair so that it billowed around her shoulders, then looked about the room with pursed lips, as if she wasn't quite sure what they were doing here, even though this bar had been her suggestion.

Sophie couldn't stop staring at her. They were related. They had to be.

"I'm Hannah," she said eventually. "I already know you're Sophie." This was almost an accusation.

Hannah wore a kind of blank expression, heightened by the heavy-lidded eye makeup, false eyelashes and the fashionably full eyebrows. Sophie got the sense that this was her normal everyday makeup and marvelled at the kind of dedication it must take to put all that on, every single day. Sophie also got the sense that the blank and guileless look Hannah wore was not an accurate reflection of her attention span, nor her intelligence.

A bartender, or maybe it was the manager, appeared at the table with a bottle of champagne. "What do you ladies say to glass of bubbly?"

"Oh, we didn't—" Sophie began.

"On the house."

"Absolutely," Hannah said. "I thought you'd never get here," she added, batting her eyelashes at him.

He proceeded to open the bottle using a lot of unnecessary hand and napkin flourishing, and a minute later, they each had glass with the rest in a bucket on the table.

Hannah raised her eyebrows to Sophie and said. "We make a good team." She held up her glass to be clinked and reluctantly, Sophie obliged, thinking *team for what?* There was a calculating glint in Hannah's eye.

Hannah took a sip of champagne then placed it on the table to give the room another dismissive glance. "We have the same dad," she said finally. "He had an affair with my mum," she added, almost cruel with her casualness, dropping the information into Sophie's awareness without preamble or preparation.

Sophie was frozen. She'd guessed this, of course. The way Hannah looked, her age, and the pre-existing knowledge that her father had been an adulterous man. It was the obvious conclusion, but still, having it said right to her face, by the actual result of her father's infidelity, was something else entirely. Sophie felt as if there was a band around her chest, growing tighter by the second.

"Look." Hannah had her phone out and was scrolling for a moment before holding it up for Sophie.

A woman, remarkably similar to Sophie's own mother, was smiling at the camera with Sophie's father beside her, his blue eyes twinkling and his sun-kissed arm slung casually over her shoulder.

Jasper Swanephol most definitely had a *type*.

Sophie cleared her throat and tried to take deep belly breaths, but panic was already rising. "Excuse me." She stood and lurched in the direction of the bathroom, managing to catch Hannah's satisfied expression as she left.

In the bathroom, she took long slow breaths. No matter how shocking, the thing that Sophie really wanted to know was what was all this about? She'd always wanted a sister. Many of her childhood fantasies had involved discovering she had a secret, long-lost sister, them becoming best friends, and going off on magical adventures together. Was this what was happening now? It didn't feel particularly magical.

After a couple of minutes of belly-breathing and nervous hand-washing Sophie pulled herself together and returned to the table. She had to at least try to be optimistic about the situation.

"Sorry... it's quite a lot to take in."

Hannah nodded graciously.

"What brings you to Auckland?"

Hannah recoiled a little, as if Sophie's question was offensive, and narrowed her eyes. "You're my sister."

"I know, but..."

"I only just found out about you." She folded her arms across her chest. "When Dad left he didn't say much. I knew he moved back here but Mum didn't tell me about his other family, uh, you and your mum, until a couple of months ago."

Suddenly Hannah's eyes filled with tears.

Sophie sat back in her chair. Her father—*their* father—Jasper, had unexpectedly shown up in Auckland nearly five years ago. They'd begun re-establishing their relationship when he had—completely out of the blue—dropped dead from a heart attack. Even with all his surfing and his lean body, it turned out that he had high cholesterol. He'd known about it, apparently, but he'd decided not to take his meds and try to cure his condition through lifestyle and mindset alone.

The manager appeared. He looked at their table and then back at the bar, then their table again. "Strange question, but you didn't happen to see a bottle of wine sitting on the bar, did you? I got it from our cellar, it's vintage, but then I took a call and now it's gone." He looked around. There were no other people in the nearby tables.

Hannah shrugged and took a sip of champagne. "Nope."

Sophie said, "No, sorry."

"Right. Okay. Well if you do…" The manager walked off, looking uncertain.

When he'd gone, Hannah leaned forward and lifted her bag up to the table. With an excited expression, she opened it a little and showed Sophie. There was a bottle of wine inside.

"That's the wine he was asking about? Why did you take it? We have all this champagne."

"This is for later," Hannah smiled, seeming pleased with herself. After a moment, realising that Sophie wasn't impressed, she narrowed her eyes. "Whatever. It's just a bottle of wine. I'm not exactly stealing from the poor."

But you are stealing, Sophie thought.

"Whatever," Hannah said, taking in Sophie's lack of enthusiasm.

For a few seconds Sophie sat there, unsure as to what she should do, then cleared her throat and said, "Hey listen, I have to go. I have a…" she wanted to say *date* but that was presumptuous. "An appointment."

"Oh my god, relax. The wine costs them like, ten bucks wholesale."

"I really have to go. I have a thing. I'll be late. Maybe we could talk later?"

Hannah regarded her sullenly. "Fine."

HARRY SHIFTED HIS weight from one leg to the other as he watched his Uber make a U-Turn on the busy K-Road and then pull up next to him.

"Western Springs Road, yeah?" The driver confirmed.

Harry nodded.

Kate lived in the downstairs apartment of a converted villa to which Harry had been a couple of times. Upstairs was a three-bedroom house, and even though Kate's flat was completely self-contained, Harry knew that she was at least on speaking terms with her neighbours.

When he got there, he took a moment to have a quick vape, and then walked down the drive to Kate's front door, which was at the side of the house. He knocked, waited, then knocked again, but the blinds were drawn and there was clearly no one home. Continuing to puff away, he walked up to the main house.

A woman in her late twenties or early thirties answered the door. "Hello?"

"Hey, uh, I'm Harry. A friend of Kate's, your downstairs neighbour? I was wondering if we could have a chat."

An hour later, Harry let himself into his own building and trudged up the stairs to his floor. The lift wasn't broken—he needed to keep moving. Just for a bit longer.

Almost as soon as he got inside his flat, the dark clouds that had been threatening all afternoon broke, and now rain was pelting down, hitting the window in a steady rhythm. Harry opened the window. Not caring that the people in the apartments across the road could see into his, or that a few droplets were finding their way inside his apartment, he peeled off his shirt and stood at the window, enjoying the feeling of cool air on his skin.

Kate's neighbour, Chloe, had noticed Kate was away and she'd been surprised about the holiday as well. She remembered Kate saying she had leave owing a while ago, but they'd bumped into each other at the mailbox a few weeks back and Kate hadn't said anything about an upcoming trip. She'd seemed distracted, though, and Chloe remembered thinking that Kate seemed as if she could do with a holiday.

But who goes on holiday and doesn't tell anyone?

Someone stressed out and fed up and wanting to get away, Harry thought. He sure as hell wouldn't mind taking off to India or somewhere.

Chloe had said she could call the landlord if he thought something was wrong but Harry had shrugged this off and left.

He was starting to feel like a paranoid freak.

Harry entered his cramped bathroom, looked longingly at the toilet for a moment, then shucked off his shoes and trousers and turned on the shower. Beads of hot water massaged his scalp and he shut his eyes to surrender to the blissful sensation. Wrapped only in a towel, he flopped onto his futon bed in the corner under the window and found himself dozing off. He let himself, not caring about a nap affecting his sleep cycles. He wouldn't be setting his alarm because he wasn't going to work tomorrow. But when he woke only twenty minutes later, he got up and pulled on a t-shirt, jeans and trainers, and headed out. It was early, but he'd find someone to talk to down the road at Verona. Not *talk*, talk, of course, just take part in the utterance and exchange of words that joined together to make sentences. It would wash over him, distract him from the knowledge that the money wasn't where it was supposed to be, and the question of why that lady who'd shown up work the other day seemed desperate to talk to him.

WITH A BEEP, Leo's phone informed him Tinder was now installed.

Now that he was hanging out with living, breathing females on a regular basis, Leo's eyes, and other body parts, had officially been reawakened. Or maybe it was that he'd stopped drinking all that coke. Either way, he'd remembered he liked girls, or women he should say, and he was acutely aware he'd been spending too much time on his own, or online in fantasy worlds, and with people like Barrett.

No more, Leo resolved. But as he swiped his way through Tinder, Leo realised very quickly that despite being the very type of person Tinder was made for, he found the whole thing rather distasteful. Not to mention intimidating. Or perhaps it was because no matter how many twenty and thirty-something women smiled at him from their Tinder profiles, he couldn't stop thinking about Alice Garnet.

WHEN SOPHIE GOT to Gypsy, Roman was already sitting at a table in the far corner.

He took one look at Sophie's glassy expression and said, "What's wrong?"

As Sophie had made the short journey from Ponsonby to West Lynn, the magnitude of what had just happened had started sinking in.

She had a *sister*.

Her father had a whole other family.

She felt numb.

"Can we order wine?"

"Of course," Roman said, a curl of worry in his stomach. Not only was he concerned about Sophie, but wine was not a good idea. It meant the lowering of inhibitions; the lowering of self-control.

But Sophie was clearly in shock.

"Do you like red?" Sophie asked.

Roman nodded.

"A bottle, please," Sophie said, pointing out an item on the menu to the bartender, who'd come over to deposit olives on their table. "And some water?"

In her shock, Sophie had become momentarily assertive.

"Will you tell me what's wrong?" Roman asked gently.

"I have a sister," she croaked. "Half-sister. The product of my dad's cheating." Sophie choked back a sob. No, she would not cry. Not here, not in front of Roman.

"Wow." Roman's eyebrows creased with concern. He reached across the table for hand but only got halfway. "Are you okay?" He studied her distressed face and added, almost to himself, "Obviously not."

The wine arrived and Roman poured them both glasses.

"My mother was the cheater in my family," he said after a moment, when it appeared Sophie was not yet ready to talk.

Sophie put down her wine, eyes wide. "You knew about it?"

Roman nodded sadly. "Virtually the whole time. My dad did too. But he couldn't leave her. She'd take off for days, leave him, us, properly...

but then come back and sweet-talk him and he'd end up taking her back." Roman shook his head.

"They're still together now?"

"No. She got worse and worse, more careless and sporadic—with both of us—and took off more and more frequently, even blatantly throwing her affairs in his face, until he was finally able to pull himself clear and we left for good. We moved here to New Zealand, when I was sixteen."

"Have you seen your mum since?" It was a relief to hear Roman talk about this, to hear about someone else's family dysfunction. But the sadness in Roman's face made her ache. At least she had been spared this. Her father had made his intentions clear when he left. Finding out about Hannah so long after it happened was shocking but in a kind of distant way. If this kind of thing had happened when she was sixteen, so fragile and vulnerable, she didn't know what she would have done.

"A few times, yes. I've made a few trips back to France." Roman took a sip of wine. "It's always a bit weird. She's my mother, but also, she's almost a stranger. And she's still the same way. All over the place and totally unreliable."

"I know what you mean. Dad came back after years and years away and it was the same. But he was trying. With me. To get to know me. Until..."

Roman frowned, waiting for Sophie to finish.

"He died," she said simply. "Heart attack. He had super high cholesterol and never got it checked because he thought he was invincible." Sophie shook her head. "Paige's dad and my dad died within three weeks of each, when we were at the start of our PhDs. It's why we..." Sophie waved her hand and Roman nodded, not needing further explanation.

"I'm sorry. About your dad."

"Thanks."

They fell silent again until Sophie said. "Have you forgiven your mum? I don't think I'd quite forgiven Dad... until he died, I guess."

Roman looked up and away for a moment, considering the question.

"I still love her, deep down. But she made us miserable with her infidelity and I don't know if I have forgiven her." He took a sip of wine and shook his head. "I'd never do that. What she did. Especially if I had a kid, you know?" His voice shook a little.

"Me neither," Sophie said, looking down.

The moment was loaded. It was so heavy Sophie almost couldn't breathe. She raised her eyes to meet Roman's. There was a sadness there. A deep, weighty sadness that Sophie didn't want to delve into. She didn't want to know whether it was about past betrayals... or something else. And so the moment hung in the air, and in the silence, the first strains of Roberta Flack's *Killing Me Softly* became audible. And despite the immensity and sadness of the moment, Sophie smiled at Roman and thought, we have a song.

# 10

At ten a.m., Sophie was still in bed.

It wasn't that she was hungover, or even particularly tired, it was that her head was a whirlwind that refused to settle. Luckily, there were no interviews scheduled today—to have to go in and be normal did not seem possible—so she would work from home. She could write up her notes from the recent interviews from right here, the comfort of her bed.

She waited until she heard Victoria—opening and closing every cupboard in the house as she got ready for work, it sounded like—and then Myra, with just the click of the front door, leave the house. She then got up herself and made a cup of coffee while her mind jumped fitfully between Hannah—what should she make of her?—and Roman. They'd said goodbye outside the bar, a slightly drunken hug in which they'd both lingered. He pulled away first and ushered her into her Uber, then waved almost wistfully as she disappeared into the night.

Sophie pressed her phone to her chest. Would he call today?

Paige was stuck in traffic, and irritation was building into a dull rage.

The day had started off well with Sophie texting to say she was working from home and that Paige should too. While Paige wasn't sure what that meant exactly, she wasn't going to press it because she was happy to have a day away from doing interviews. When she'd started getting bored, she'd tried pretending she was interrogating suspects, but it had become obvious that this wasn't a suitable approach. Hopefully, a day off interviews would renew her enthusiasm. It also meant she could run a few errands and check up on Hazel.

But now, her good mood had well and truly disappeared. Where were all these people going in their cars? Why weren't they tucked up at work somewhere instead of getting in Paige's way? She exhaled noisily and leaned on her horn to communicate her frustration, as drivers tend to do, even though its only effect was to thoroughly annoy the people in surrounding cars.

Paige now regretted her jaunt to the bank. Her appointment had been with Mr Scofield, and she'd set it up for the sole purpose of saying *I told you so*. She had, of course, couched this childish sentiment in a sensible financial discussion about loans etc., but Mr Scofield had gotten the point because Paige was about as subtle as a brick wall.

When Paige had initially met with him a few months ago to procure a small business loan for S & S Investigations, he, only just middle-aged but apparently unfamiliar with the idea of Girl Power, or even Feminism, had listened to her pitch with a patronising smile, finally saying that it was a preposterous idea, but he would approve the loan because of her mother's long standing relationship with the bank and, presumably, her healthy account balance. Now that they'd solved two cases and had a new corporate gig, she hadn't been able to resist scheduling a follow-up visit to throw it gleefully in Mr Scofield's face. It did not occur to Paige that this was perhaps foolish, given there were no assurances of ongoing work. No, Paige was an optimist, and she felt sure that their business was now taking off.

Finally, the traffic began to move and five minutes later, Paige was pulling into a park just down the road from S & S Investigations. Would Hazel be there, she wondered as she ascended the stairs? No, the door was closed and the office was dark.

Paige let herself into S & S and sat at her desk, taking a moment to happily regard her surroundings. It didn't matter that it was a little old-fashioned, even shabby, with out-of-date décor. It made it seem more authentic. Paige wondered about those renovations Hazel mentioned, before realising that if Hazel was having issues with memory and confusion, maybe she'd forgotten to organise them. With a sigh, Paige put the matter out of her head. She'd have to wait until she next saw Hazel and hope that they could have a proper conversation.

Paige opened her laptop and then picked up the landline phone to check voicemail. She was thrilled when the robotic voice told her there was one message, but when she called back it turned out to be a wrong number. Paige asked the person how they could have listened to the entire outgoing message, stating that the caller had reached S & S Investigations and no case was too big or small, without twigging that this was not a company that sold office supplies, and then hung up. She turned her attention to the online news site, scanning the stories for a potential lead—this had been how they got the Dixon case, after all—but there was nothing that even Paige could turn into a case. Plus, did they even have the capacity to take on more work? Paige was doing this out of habit rather than need. But if they did have another case they could split up the work and then give Leo something proper to do. Paige sat up straighter. And even hire an assistant or associate or something.

But the news yielded no potential cases and so she turned her attention to writing up interview notes, as Sophie had suggested.

At almost precisely two o'clock, Paige stopped working and nipped downstairs to grab something for lunch. After a bit of back and forth between her two favourite places within twenty metres of the office, she decided on a chicken and parmesan panini from the place on the corner. She was unlocking the door to her office, her takeaway bag tucked under one arm, when someone cleared their throat behind her.

"Can I help you?" Paige called out over her shoulder as she entered the office and deposited her food on her desk.

"I hope so."

He was in his late thirties, or maybe forties, Paige thought as he got closer. His clothes suggested some sort of professional skateboarder, but there were noticeable lines on his face.

"My name's Eddie. My aunt is Hazel, across the hall?" Paige nodded. "Listen, you haven't seen her today, have you?"

"Hazel? No, why?" Paige's chest felt unexpectedly tight.

"She's not at home, or in her office, and we were supposed to meet for lunch. I don't know where she is."

"You've tried calling?"

"Of course. She'd left me a message, but it didn't make sense." Eddie's worried face studied hers. "You don't know where she is?"

Should she tell him what she'd seen, Paige wondered. He was her family, of course she should. He was clearly worried about her. And she might be missing.

"You'd better sit down," Paige said.

In between mouthfuls of panini, she recounted the periods of confusion she'd recently observed in Hazel. Eddie nodded gravely and told her that he'd first wondered if something was wrong when she came to stay with them. His mother, her sister, had been deathly sick—the reason Hazel went back to Dunedin—and Hazel had stayed until the end.

"Wait. Her sister is dead? She said something about hearing her voice."

Eddie shook his head sadly. "She may have been hallucinating. While she was in Dunedin I noticed a few things. Here and there and kind of all over the place, you know?" Eddie said. "After Mum, uh, passed, I offered to come up here with her, and to help with odd jobs, but it was really to keep an eye on her."

"Huh," Paige said.

"And I think it's getting worse. Recently, it seems as if," Eddie paused, looking pained, "I think it might be dementia," he finished with a weary exhalation.

SOPHIE COULDN'T BELIEVE it. Hannah had texted her to demand an explanation for leaving yesterday. Where did she get the nerve, and why hadn't Sophie inherited that particular gene? Sophie didn't answer the message—she had no idea what to say—but found herself instead, her breath catching in her throat as she did so, messaging Roman with an update.

He responded straight away.

*Has she told you why she contacted you yet?*

*No. She seems...angry with me or something.*

*You want me to look her up?*

As Sophie was thinking, yes, absolutely, Roman added a winky face. Did that mean his offer had been a joke? Either way, she couldn't do that, it would be pretty over the top to ask your policeman friend to run a background check on your recently discovered sister.

*Thanks for listening last night. It really helped.*

*My pleasure.*

Sophie watched as the three little dots told her Roman was typing something else. The dots disappeared. Nothing. They reappeared, then finally, Roman's message came through.

*Have to shoot off now but catch up later. I still have to tell you what I found in an old case file.*

Sophie looked at her phone with disappointment.

LEO AND ALICE had made short work of the weeds in Alice's back garden and were halfway through the new project Alice had dreamed up—a vegetable patch. While they tilled the soil they chatted easily, and sooner rather than later, the subject of Leo's love life came up. Leo told Alice, rather forlornly, that he was single but not voluntarily.

"Well now," Alice waved coyly at Leo, moving her hand to play with the hair at the nape of her neck, curling with the heat, "surely there must be one nice girl who you fancy on Tinder?"

"The ones my age are... I don't know."

Despite his limited experience with women, Leo's approach of simply saying what was on his mind—his thoughts were generally of a flattering nature—was remarkably effective.

It was certainly working with Alice.

She turned back and poked at the soil, feeling rather warm and finding it hard to concentrate. Society as a whole may not be *quite* ready for this kind of relationship, but in practicality it worked rather well. Leo needed a mentor-type figure in his life, someone to tell him things and teach him how to be a grown-up, essentially. His own mother would have been happy to do this, but had somehow never managed to transition from mothering him to mentoring him. Both she and her husband, as parents seemed to do nowadays, hadn't taken off Leo's training wheels and had spent far too many of his adult years running after him holding the handlebars and assuring him that yes, they were still holding on.

But now, it appeared Leo might have Alice to teach him about the ways of the world. And this was a much better arrangement. For both of them.

TomTom appeared from the shrubbery at the side of the house and sauntered over to Leo, winding himself around his legs and purring. It almost seemed as if TomTom remembered Leo. He certainly appeared rather pleased to see him. Perhaps he remembered the expensive food Leo had purchased in a desperate attempt to keep his kidnapped pets happy. Leo tried to push him away with his foot—gently—but TomTom's purring grew even louder and rolled over onto his back. He rather liked this playfulness.

Leo cast a furtive glance at Alice. Had she noticed?

But luckily for Leo, she had not. Alice was staring dreamily into the distance.

"This reminds me of the summer I spent in Rome," she said. "My OE after seventh form."

Lifting bags of soil and sweating over a garden was nothing like her summer in Rome—the only lifting she'd done was to transport espressos, wine and cigarettes to her lips, and the only sweating had been with the local waiter, tangled between the sheets—but she wanted Leo to know she was the type of sophisticated, cosmopolitan woman that could throw out sentences like that. Alice glanced over at Leo to see if he was impressed. He was.

# 11

The next day Harry had still not returned to work.

There was nothing for it, Sophie thought resolutely, she'd have to speak to his manager and find out what was going on. She opened the door to her room to find Sharon nervously hovering outside.

"Hi, Sharon. Are you meeting with Paige again?"

She shook her head. "No, I just…"

Sophie waited, but Sharon didn't finish her thought.

"Everything okay?"

"I'm worried I made a bad impression. From my interview."

"I'm sure you were fine."

"Really?"

Sophie nodded reassuringly even though Paige had told her that of the interviews she'd done so far, Sharon seemed to have the least clue as to what she was supposed to be doing. But Sophie did not want to start worrying about another employee when she had Harry to think about.

"Listen, while I have you, can you tell me who I can talk to about Harry?"

"Harry King? Well, you can ask me—" Sharon bit her lip. "Michelle is the payroll manager, maybe talk to her?"

"Thank you."

"I'll show you the way."

Before Sophie could tell Sharon this wasn't necessary, she was bustling her along to the lift. On the eighth floor, Sharon led Sophie toward an office and inside, Sophie realised that Harry's manager was the woman in the charcoal suit who'd been listening to Sophie's conversation last week. The one Sophie thought was cosy with Josh.

"She and Josh had a thing a few months ago," Sharon whispered in Sophie's ear, as if reading Sophie's mind.

"Thanks Sharon. I'll let you get back to work now, okay?"

"Oh, of course. Yes." Sharon nodded, blushed, and then hurried away.

Sophie knocked on the open office door. "Hello? Sorry to bother you."

Michelle was wearing another beautiful suit, this one inky black and completely wrinkle free, and paired with the most beautiful pair of skin-coloured suede boots Sophie had ever seen.

Michelle blinked at Sophie, then cleared her throat and stood. "Michelle." She held out her hand for Sophie to shake. "You're from the company doing the psychometric testing?" she asked as Sophie took a seat.

"Yes, although that isn't quite why I'm here."

"Right, right." Michelle nodded, clasping her hands together in front of her. Her eyes travelled over Sophie as if she was weighing up 'the competition'. Sophie wanted to assure Michelle that she was not at all interested in Josh, but it didn't seem appropriate.

"I'm here to talk about your direct report, Harry."

Michelle swallowed and licked her lips. "Yes?"

"I'm worried. He seems really stressed out, and now he's not at work."

Michelle turned to her computer and quickly typed something. Sophie was impressed by how fast she could type with such long fingernails.

"He's away sick." Michelle turned back to Sophie. "What makes you think there's something wrong?"

"It's hard to explain. He... he seems very on edge. As if he's not coping."

"How many times did you meet with him?"

"Only twice."

"Harry is a rather edgy young man on any given day. And I do wonder whether he gets enough sleep, or eats properly... you know what young men living on their own are like."

Sophie shrugged, unconvinced. "I guess."

Michelle eyed her for a moment, as if deciding whether or not to confide in Sophie. "Between you and me?" Michelle leaned forward. She waited for Sophie to nod before continuing. "I think Harry may be using drugs. Probably only on the weekend, but I do wonder whether it is starting to affect his work. I'd already made of a note of it, something to follow up on, but I wanted to give him a chance to pull himself together before doing anything formal."

Sophie sat back in her chair, processing this information as she mentally ran through all her interactions with Harry. Yes. His behaviour and demeanour were consistent with drug use.

"When he returns to the office, I'm going to call him in and suggest he seek counselling or enter a rehab programme." Michelle nodded, her eyes wide with concern.

Sophie thought that Michelle was hamming up the concern to a level beyond what was genuine, but still, as explanations went, this checked all the Harry boxes. She sighed and stood up. "Thank you for your time. I hope Harry gets better soon."

"Oh, one more thing?" Michelle called before Sophie left the office. "Will you be making a note of your concerns on his file? The file you have for your testing?"

"Should I?"

Michelle nodded. "Yes, I think it would be prudent to note such reflections. That is part of the reason we have you doing this, after all."

Sophie felt a little sick as she left Michelle's office. Had she gotten Harry into trouble? No, she shook her head, trying to convince herself. Michelle said she was already aware of the problem. Sophie had merely voiced a concern. And this way, he'd get help. Still, Sophie thought as she pushed the elevator button, she couldn't help but feel like a bit of a nark.


PAIGE WAS WORRIED.

Even though Hazel had returned home safe and sound after she went missing for those few hours the other day, Eddie had just texted to say Hazel had had another spell of disorientation and they seemed to be increasing. He said there was no reason to be alarmed, he was just letting her know, but this wasn't enough for Paige. She wanted to see for herself. She wanted to help. But she didn't know where Hazel lived, and even if she did, she couldn't very well show up there and demand… what? Some sort of medical consultation? And Eddie was taking her to the doctors tomorrow anyway, he said. Really, this had nothing to do with Paige. Eddie was Hazel's family, and he was aware of what was going on, so it was all in hand.

But this did not make Paige feel better, it made her feel helpless. She wasn't quite sure why she was so invested in this woman—she hadn't even known Hazel a few weeks ago—but nevertheless, she was. Perhaps it was because Hazel seemed to Paige as if she could be the grandmother she never had. Her father's parents had died when Paige was young, before any real bond could develop, and her mother's mother lived in England and was apparently so awful that Paige should consider herself lucky she'd never met her.

Unable to ignore the pangs of hunger that had been building for at least an hour, Paige exited the office and scuttled down to the place on the corner to get another one of those chicken paninis. When she saw a four-person queue inside, she hesitated—she didn't have time to wait—but only for a moment. Everyone waiting in line was looking intently at their phone. Without further contemplation, she ambled up to the counter, loitered casually behind the woman currently giving her order, and stepped into her place once she moved away. The man who had been next in line looked up, frowned at his miscalculation—hadn't he been next?—then shrugged to himself and returned to his phone.

Back in the office Paige flicked through Instagram as she ate her panini. Suddenly she stopped, nearly choking on the bite she'd just taken. What the hell was she looking at? Her mother, her *mother*, was in a selfie with Leo on his Instagram. She was smiling coyly up at the camera, held high by Leo, her face flushed and smudged with soil.

The garden behind them appeared to be coming along nicely.

Paige scrutinized the photo and nearly exclaimed out loud when she noticed an extra detail. Her mother's top button was undone. Her mother was showing actual cleavage.

*WTF.*


SOPHIE COULDN'T LET it go.

Even if the way Harry was acting was because of a drug problem, that didn't mean someone shouldn't be trying to help him. It was maybe even more of a reason. Deep in thought, Sophie wandered from her meeting room to the breakroom for a coffee to help her think. As she neared the entrance, she spotted Sharon sitting on the edge of someone's desk talking animatedly.

The town gossip was exactly the person she needed.

"Sorry to interrupt," she said, approaching the desk. "Sharon, can I borrow you for a sec?"

"Absolutely." Sharon hopped off the edge of the desk, delighted, and followed Sophie into the tearoom.

With a cup of tea in hand and an eager smile on her face, Sharon provided Sophie with a long-winded story of which the gist was that she didn't know Harry very well but he seemed like an okay guy.

"Oh, and he's off sick at the moment. The timing is terrible with Kate on leave and another payroll run coming up, but these things happen." She shrugged.

"Kate?"

"Kate Brodie. She's in payroll with Harry. She's on annual leave." Sharon paused and looked contemplative. "You know, I don't even know where she's gone. Maybe her holiday was unplanned." She took a sip of tea. "But it can't have been completely spontaneous, you can't just up and leave work without submitting the proper forms."

"Are Kate and Harry friends?"

"It seemed like they were friendly, yes. They eat lunch together regularly."

Something flickered across Sharon's face, and Sophie wondered if Sharon was realising that she didn't routinely have lunch with people, but then Sharon shrugged and smiled.

"Can I ask something a bit delicate?" Sophie said, hoping that she wasn't causing more problems for Harry by talking to Sharon.

Sharon leaned forward, almost breathless with anticipation.

"Do you think Harry was stressed?"

Sharon made a thinking face and then shook her head.

"No, um…" Sophie paused "other issues? Like…"

"Drugs?" Sharon hissed, leaning forward before sitting back. "I thought I heard a whisper a while back, but I thought it couldn't be. He seems so quiet. He's not into the P is he? I've read all about that. It's always in the papers, isn't it?"

"Well, no, I don't think he's taking methamphetamine, I mean…"

Sophie trailed off, feeling guilty and foolish. What on earth was she doing, bringing someone like Sharon into this?

"Sorry, listen. Forget I said anything, okay?"

Sharon nodded eagerly and Sophie left the tearoom with the awful feeling she'd made Harry's life more difficult.

Twenty minutes later, Sharon came rushing into Sophie's meeting room, eyes wide and cheeks flushed.

"The police were here," she gushed. "They spoke to Josh."

"They did?" Sophie found that she'd stood up. "Why?"

"To tell him about Kate."

"The payroll clerk."

Sharon nodded, her chin wobbling with excitement. "And because Harry's office number was the last number Kate dialled."

"What do you mean the last number?" Sophie said, her voice quiet.

"It was him apparently," she carried on, her face flushing even redder. "Harry."

"*What* was Harry?" Sophie was now clutching the edge of the desk.

"He went around to Kate's house and talked to the neighbour. He asked if she'd seen Kate and after he left, the neighbour thought about it and got worried. She called the landlord and they went inside and that's when they found her."

Sophie waited, dread washing over her shoulders.

"Dead."

# 12

It was an accident, as it turned out. Kate had somehow stumbled over her rucksack, which she appeared to be in the process of packing, and hit her head on the heavy oak coffee table in the middle of the living room. It all had to be confirmed by the coroner, of course, but there was no indication it was anything other than a tragic turn of events.

But why had Harry gone over there. Why had he felt the need to check on her and talk to her neighbour? Sophie bit the inside of her lip and strolled from her bedroom to the kitchen to wash out her coffee cup and put it in the dishwasher.

"Sophie, are you ready?" Victoria called from the hallway.

"Um. Okay."

Victoria was insisting on indoctrinating Myra to the wonders of the weekend Farmer's Market and Sophie, needing a break from her own thoughts, had agreed to come—especially since it appeared Victoria was going to focus her attention on Myra.

An hour later, after they'd done one circuit together, Victoria dragged Myra away to the organic smoothie place so that she could inflict her favourite kale-and-something concoction on her. Sophie sidled away happily to purchase a bag of avocados. What kind of avocado-based meal could she make tonight, she wondered. She ambled toward a nut stand and eyed the various options— perhaps some sort of fancy salad—until something made her look up.

It was a mere glimpse from afar; a familiar shape. Sophie focused her attention and craned her neck. There it was again. A profile she knew. Sophie smiled as her stomach did a happy flip.

It was Roman.

He was here.

But when Sophie realised what she was actually looking at, she was so utterly unprepared it was as if a bomb had gone off right next to her and she'd been sent flying through the air.

Ten metres in front of her was Roman. Next to him was a woman who Sophie knew instantly was his wife. There was something proprietary about the space between them, even though they weren't touching. It hung around them, like a cloud. Or a stench. Years of history and shared experience. Love?

Shock rushed through Sophie's body and landed with a thump in her stomach.

Roman was married.

The woman was tall, somewhere between willowy and lanky, with the kind of reddish, strawberry-blonde hair Sophie had always wanted. It swished around her shoulders in loose bouncy curls, whereas Sophie's fell in boring brown clumps. The woman looked like she did yoga but also drank wine, so she wasn't aggressively and annoyingly healthy, and she gave the impression of floating about life without feeling stupid or unsure about anything.

Roman's eyes found Sophie's. He paled. A brief flit of something—pain? apology?—crossed his face. He took a step forward and raised his hand. Sophie stepped backward, hit something solid and felt it yield. A second later, she'd lost her centre of gravity and was on the ground surrounded by an assortment of organic, packaged nuts.

"Are you okay?" The owner of the stand was helping Sophie to her feet, but all she could see was Roman, now standing in front of her. The woman, his wife, looked at Sophie, her eyes narrowing, and looped her hand through Roman's elbow. Roman looked down at this gesture, surprise knitting his brows as if it was unfamiliar, or at least unexpected, then lifted his eyes to Sophie.

"You're alright?" he asked as Sophie managed to get upright.

"Uh, y-yes." Sophie felt numb. Watching them was like watching a different person live out her life.

"I'm Anya," the woman said. "Roman's wife," she added pointedly.

Sophie didn't have the strength to introduce herself.

"Ah..." Roman said in the silence. "Anya, this is... Dr Swanephol. She's... ah... she and her partner own an investigation agency. We worked on a case together."

Anya pulled Roman closer to her. "Roman drags me to these things," she murmured languidly. "But it's a lovely day to be out and about."

Sophie felt a yearning so intense she thought she might choke.

"We'd better head off, we're going to brunch. Nice to meet you." Anya steered Roman away. He turned back to make eye contact but Anya tugged his arm again.

They were gone in seconds, but it felt like an eternity before they were out of Sophie's sight, and for that eternity she stood there with wind roaring in her ears and blood pounding in her chest as everything collapsed in a pile at her feet.

SOPHIE WENT STRAIGHT to her bedroom, ignoring Myra's questions and Victoria's persistent knocking. She pulled on her grey tracksuit pants, slipped on her headphones, put on Amy Winehouse, and crawled into bed.

Of course he had a wife. How had she not seen all the clues? The red indent on his finger was so fresh. It was obvious now that his ring was only off temporarily because of recent weight gain. All of his clothes had seemed a little ill-fitting and he didn't seem like the kind of guy to indulge in that skin-tight-suit look. Sophie sighed. For some reason she found a weakness like this, one she could relate to, endearing. It did make her wonder though, why he'd put on weight. Was he stressed? And if so, was it work, or was it his home life? There had been something strained between him and Anya today. Her overt display of affection had seemed awkward. Roman had even flinched slightly when she'd looped her arm in his. He'd definitely looked a little surprised. But maybe she was misremembering, Sophie thought. And what did it even matter, Sophie chastised herself.

Roman was married.


ALICE HAD PREPARED a lovely platter of bread and cold cuts for their lunch, and she served this with a decanted half-litre of wine.

"What's all this?" Leo said as he emerged from the bathroom, looking delighted at the feast in front of him.

"No trouble." Alice smiled.

The weather had looked promising in the morning so Alice had called Leo to ask if he wanted to work on the garden today, but after a productive couple of hours, the sky had turned dark and rain seemed imminent, so they decided to abandon their gardening for lunch inside.

Alice looked pointedly at Leo's hands and raised her eyebrows. Leo blushed and turned and scuttled back to wash up properly. By the time Leo re-emerged from the bathroom with a waft of white jasmine hand soap, Alice had lit a candle and set the table. The whole thing was so classy and charming Leo felt as if he was in a movie.

"Here's a plate, and a napkin. The bread is all cut... of course so is the meat. I thought we could help ourselves... make sandwiches, or..."

Alice seemed shy, almost uncertain, and Leo, suddenly feeling confident, picked up the wine and poured them each a healthy-sized glass.

"Cheers," he said, holding up his glass. "Thanks for this... opportunity... I don't know the last time I've had such a good time with somebody."

They both took large mouthfuls of wine and busied themselves with napkins and plates and selecting ingredients for their sandwiches. Leo finished his first in record speed. He was hungry, but also nervous, and was about to reach for another chunk of ciabatta when he paused, wondering if he was coming across as a big, oafish pig.

"Yes, have another," Alice said, both her eyes and her voice, warm.

"Oh, I don't know—"

"Honestly, please." Alice reached out to select a piece of bread for him at the same time as Leo did. Their hands touched. They held each other's gaze. The moment hung, still as a windless day, until both Alice and Leo, each emboldened by 250 mls of Chianti, leaned closer to one another. Alice fluttered her eyelashes, tilted her head a fraction, and Leo kissed her.

A COUPLE OF hours later, Sophie woke up from a nap with the horrible sick feeling of being disturbed in the middle of a deep sleep—or maybe it was waking up with that exhausted feeling when you know you've been crying.

Sophie needed a distraction. She slouched out of bed, retrieved her laptop from her desk, and returned to bed to check her emails. Well, she thought, she'd asked and the universe had provided. There was a distraction of a most unpleasant kind waiting in her inbox.

She had to give a presentation.

A wave of dread surged through her body. It was incredible how the brain could release such an immediate flood of stress hormones. She felt almost light-headed as she blinked and re-read Josh's email. He'd been out of the office on Friday at a planning weekend with the execs, but had managed to find the time to message her and request an update on the psychometric testing. They needed to start making some decisions on the restructuring and they'd like the *girls* to present what they'd found so far on Tuesday.

Tuesday!

Sophie's stomach folded in on itself. She forwarded the email to Paige, adding a couple of exclamation marks and then started a new document and wondered what on earth they could present to them.

Her phone rang.

It was Roman.

She couldn't bring herself to answer it; she couldn't listen to his traitorous voice. She couldn't bear to hear him ask her how she was, then try to explain. There was no explanation necessary. He was married and he hadn't told her. He'd let her feel the way she felt. Or had she imagined the whole thing? It didn't even matter. Either way, she felt like an idiot and a loser and like she needed to do something to wash away the bitter taste of betrayal in her mouth. She needed to get on with things, forge ahead, conquer new domains... or something.

Sophie pulled out her phone and re-installed Tinder. As she waited, she pushed her feet into her slippers, stood up, and shuffled out of her room into the living room. She threw her phone on the sofa and went into the kitchen to get a glass of water.

"Sophie? Are you back on Tinder?"

It was Myra, the semi-corporeal flatmate, emerging from the shadows.

"Hi, uh, yeah." Sophie didn't elaborate and flopped onto the couch.

She felt like *such* an idiot for the fantasies she had already indulged in. Fat lot of good her PhD had done her in real life. Behavioural expert my *ass*, thought Sophie. She couldn't even pick up a basic clue like his marital status. And she was supposed to be an investigator. Sophie bit back a bitter laugh. Speaking of fat asses... did they have any ice-cream? She didn't even care if it wasn't hers, she'd face Victoria's wrath if she had to.

Sophie pulled herself up. She was about to return to the kitchen to investigate when the front door slammed. High-heels clip-clopped down the hallway. Victoria was home. The footsteps continued past Victoria's room, seeming to get more aggressive as they got nearer. Sophie winced at the sound. They were all supposed to take heeled shoes off by the front door, they had a shoe rack and everything. This rule had been raised—ironically by Victoria, after Sophie had worn high heels in the house—and agreed upon by the three of them, many months ago.

"Oh. Hi." Victoria seemed displeased that both her flatmates were home, and, of all the audacity, had already turned on the TV and selected something to watch.

"Hey," Sophie said, suddenly reminded of the ominous landlord visit. "Did you ever find out why the landlord came to visit?" Sophie asked.

Victoria shrugged, uninterested. "Just an inspection."

A glimmer of hope flickered in Sophie's belly. Perhaps at least she could take getting kicked out of her flat off her list of Things To Worry/Be Miserable About.

Victoria nodded, but she wasn't listening. She'd also noticed that Sophie's phone, lying abandoned on the couch, was open on Tinder.

"Ooh, Tinder," Victoria said with considerably more pep. "Are we on Tinder at the same time?"

"I am," Myra said quietly.

Sophie looked over Myra's shoulder. Sure enough, her phone was also open on the dating app.

Sophie shrugged. "I guess we are."

"Wait for me." Victoria tottered off to her room, unstable on her super high heels. They were the same heels she'd worn to the ball the other night, so Sophie suspected they were shockingly expensive and she was wearing them to work to get her money's worth. Or perhaps someone had complimented her on them. Sophie, still looking in the direction that Victoria had gone, recalled that the night of the ball, Victoria hadn't come home until the morning, and rather bizarrely had kept quiet on the subject. Perhaps she'd had such a bad night even she couldn't re-arrange it so that it fit her personal narrative of being popular.

Victoria emerged from her room clutching her phone and wearing leggings and a singlet with a long cardigan. "God, Soph. You look like crap.

What's wrong with you?" she said as she sailed past Sophie into the kitchen. She turned back to add, "You really need to think about changing your skin regime."

"Thanks," Sophie said under her breath.

Victoria returned a few minutes later, her eyes bright with excitement. "Wine and nibbles? I've got cheese and crackers and some other stuff."

When she wasn't measuring the levels of her labelled almond milk and leaving notes insinuating it was lower than it should be, Victoria could be quite generous. On the rare occasions that they hung out as flatmates she always provided expensive wine and uncharacteristically refused any offers to pay her back. But Victoria's generosity was only ever on her own terms and had to serve her in some way.

They settled in with cheese, crackers, sundried tomatoes and pesto, plus a bottle of Pinot Gris which had already been chilling in the fridge, and started swiping. Being different ages, physical types, and with different profile styles, there didn't tend to be a lot of crossover in the matches of the three flatmates.

Myra, cute and clearly shy, was a magnet for guys who described themselves as easy-going, but in reality only opted for girls who seemed like they wouldn't put up much of a fight when it came to making decisions, or who would fit into their own life without any sort of accommodation on their part. Victoria, with long blonde hair and a trout-pout perfected for the camera, got a fair amount of Tinder attention from guys that Sophie avoided like the plague, but Victoria seemed to like. Sophie generally matched with anyone she'd swiped right. Her unassuming expression combined with her beautiful face seemed to inspire—in all sorts of men—wild fantasies about who Sophie was and who she could be to them, exacerbating even the slightest tendency for delusion.

"I think I might be interested in older men, you know? Guys my age seem so immature," Victoria said out of the blue.

Sophie had a sneaking suspicion that this was related to Victoria's obvious interest in Professor Richard Thinton. What on earth did she see in him, Sophie wondered. He of course wasn't ugly, but she thought his personality so odious that it transformed his neutral features and normal face into something rather off-putting.

Not wanting to encourage Victoria, Sophie didn't say anything and returned to scrolling through Tinder. After a few minutes she shook her head. "If an alien came down and used Tinder to assess the human heterosexual male population—in New Zealand at least—they would think owning a dog, going fishing, driving a car or a motorbike, and travelling, or at least hiking, were the absolute cornerstone of male existence." She said, then thought to herself, maybe they are. "Where are the photos of a guy reading a book, or like, eating a yummy dinner or something?"

Victoria snorted, then said, "Ugh, listen to this. *If you don't look like your photo, you'll be buying drinks until you do.*"

"Wow. He might as well have written *judgemental wanker* in his profile description," Sophie said.

Myra giggled.

They each continued to tap and scroll, sharing the worst and best of the profiles.

"Hehe... here's one..." Victoria showed the others a profile of a guy wearing nothing except for a woollen beanie and a cheeky smile. He was lying on his stomach and the camera angle, a selfie, offered the viewer a tantalising view of the top of his bottom—a feat which, Sophie thought, must have involved rather a lot of back arching. They all laughed but Sophie saw Victoria swipe right.

"Here, look," Sophie held up her phone for the other two. His profile photo was a picture of a large snapper. "The fishing one gets me the most. I mean, do guys realise how unappealing fishing is? I mean, doesn't it mean they're off with their mates all weekend on fishing trips?" Sophie eyed the photo. "He must be trying to convey his ability to provide food for his woman... unless he is in fact, a fish."

"Check out this mysterious one." Victoria showed them a profile with seven photos, each of which the guy was wearing a hat and sunglasses. "Married?"

Sophie and Myra nodded. "Married."

At this word Sophie felt a surge of unhappiness, but she quickly pushed it down. She was not feeling miserable right now and she didn't want that to change.

"*This* guy's entire description is made up of emojis," Sophie said. She went through the rest of the profile, sipping her wine. "I have a theory about emoji use," she added, "the more emojis a guy uses, the less emotionally available he is."

"Sounds about right," said Victoria.

"I have one," Myra said in a small voice.

"Go ahead." Sophie smiled in encouragement.

Myra read out a profile description in which the guy aggressively stated that he wasn't interested in anyone's baggage; that anyone with baggage or issues should immediately go away and look elsewhere; that he didn't want a high maintenance chick or any gold-diggers... It went on.

"It sounds like he's the one with baggage," Sophie said with an eye roll.

They didn't spend all their time laughing at profiles, they also shared promising matches, cute profiles, and people they thought they might know from somewhere. All in all, it had been a fun night, Sophie thought as she changed for bed with a slightly fuzzy head. She had four matches which she would peruse tomorrow without the influence of wine to affect her perception. She filled up her bottle of water, glugging it back even as she climbed into bed, placed it on the nightstand, and as she reached over to get her book to read a chapter before bed, the deep melancholy cloaking her earlier in the day suddenly re-appeared. It crept back in, sneaking up from her toes, slowly steadily, making its way through her entire body until it had engulfed her completely.

One hot, fat, tear, slid down her cheek, and then another. As she dropped her book at the side of the bed and leaned over to turn out the light she started sobbing. She felt as if she was sixteen again, utterly miserable over a boy who would never be hers.

ROMAN, SITTING PROPPED up against the headboard, took a controlled breath and looked over at Anya who was lying beside him.

"You uploaded those photos from our trip to Queenstown?"

"Yes?" Anya didn't look up.

"It was three years ago."

Anya kept scrolling through her Facebook feed. "They've already gotten heaps of comments and likes."

"But why now?"

Anya shrugged.

Roman thought he knew the answer, but to say it would be admitting something he couldn't bring himself to raise. Since they'd bumped into Sophie at the Farmer's Market, Anya had been affectionate and sweet. She'd insisted they have a date night this evening, and she'd even cooked him a special dinner. This flurry of romance was in stark contrast to the indifference that had crept into their marriage over the last few years. Apparently, if anything could revive Anya's interest in Roman it was competition. At the very least a flame of jealousy had been ignited by Sophie's appearance.

Roman again looked over at Anya, who was scrolling through photos on Instagram. The glow from her tablet illuminated her reddish-blonde hair and danced across her high cheekbones. Outwardly she'd hardly changed over their seven-year marriage, but she seemed so different now. Sometimes she felt like a stranger. They'd had good times together. Certainly at the beginning, before she'd realised he loved his job but wasn't aiming to become the youngest police commissioner in New Zealand; and before she realised what kind of lifestyle a policeman's salary meant in the expensive city of Auckland.

"What?" Anya made an annoyed sound in the back of throat but kept her eyes fixed on her device.

"Nothing," Roman said, and went back to his book.

But he couldn't concentrate.

He couldn't rid himself of the look on Sophie's face when she'd seen them at the market. It made his stomach clench and, if Roman was completely honest with himself, his heart ache. Sophie had been crushed, and while a part of him soared at the knowledge that she felt that way, that he hadn't been wrong about their connection, the cold hard reality was that he was in fact, a married man.

# 13

The next morning, Sophie reached down and pulled her laptop onto the surface of her bed.

What was the earliest you could get pizza delivered, she wondered.

Interviews had been suspended for a couple of days while the HR department mourned the loss of one of their team, so this Monday morning Sophie would be remaining in bed. They still had to give their presentation—the executives were busy people and rescheduling was not an option—but that was tomorrow. She texted Paige and said she wasn't coming into the office, but she'd start the first draft of the presentation and send it through to Paige for review. They could dedicate tomorrow morning to finishing it off and having a few run-throughs. Paige agreed. Sophie, now having two hours to kill before she could start her pizza-and-

Netflix-based wallowing session, made a strong pot of coffee and started on the presentation. At nearly midday, she sent what she'd done to Paige, ordered her pizza, and checked out her Netflix options. Something heart-breaking, she decided. She wanted to have a good cry now so tears wouldn't spring up later at some inappropriate moment. What was that one with Daenerys Targaryen in it, Sophie mused, about looking after someone who was sick? Or the YA one about the terminally ill girl? After finding both and deciding she'd watch one after the other, Sophie settled into the rest of her day.

On Tuesday morning, she took a colder than comfortable shower, slapped on more makeup than normal, chose a crisp white shirt and a simple black-and-white skirt, and headed to the office.

Paige was already there.

"Hey," she said. "How's it going? You ready to nail this presentation?"

"Hhnngh," Sophie mumbled.

"You okay?" Paige, staring at Sophie's face. "Are you still thinking about that payroll clerk?"

Sophie shrugged and made a so-so gesture. The Harry and Kate situation was still on her mind but it had been momentarily displaced by the shock of seeing Roman with his wife. For a moment she considered telling Paige, but instead she said, "Didn't sleep well." She couldn't dredge those feelings up again, she just couldn't.

And they had work to do.

"Let's go into the conference room," Paige suggested, standing up and taking her laptop through with her. Sophie followed her in. "Thanks for the draft. I made a few changes and added some more background stuff. What we need now is to write up our methods and get some actual data to present. I can do a data extract from the system if you're happy to write up the methods?"

"Sure," Sophie replied.

For a couple of hours they worked quietly, with the only sounds in the office the clacking of their keyboards and the refilling of coffee.

"Okay," Paige said eventually, sitting back. "We don't have enough data to run tests through a statistical analysis programme, but we can still describe the sample. What do we want to tell them?"

This type of presentation was in neither Paige nor Sophie's wheelhouse.

"Ooh, I know." Sophie said, starting to look enthusiastic. Writing up research methods had always been something she enjoyed, and on top of that it was successfully distracting her from the unpleasant thoughts and emotions still humming below the surface. "We could use a case study. I've got the perfect person in mind."

"Is it Sharon and her complete lack of awareness of what she's supposed to be doing? Or that her most highly honed skill is her ability to waste time?"

Sophie shook her head. "I don't want to shine a spotlight on her and get her fired. No, I've got a more interesting one."

She told Paige about McKenna—the possible case of narcissistic personality disorder—and how her personality was a classic mismatch to her role, and worse, probably had a detrimental effect on the rest of the team's productivity, or at the very least morale. And one team could then go on to influence the overall department culture and climate.

"We won't say her name, of course, that wouldn't be fair, but it would be a great way to show how these results can be used to inform hiring practices."

Paige grinned. "If you write it up, I'll say the words," she said.

"Perfect," Sophie replied.

They smiled at each other, both thinking that they were indeed a great team.

"The case study could go after the method, the explanation of what tests and interviews we're conducting," Sophie said.

"Yeah, and then we could explain what we would do once all the data has been collected, look at the culture of the department, and stuff like that," Paige added. "And I'll throw in a bit of psychobabble. A bit of razzle dazzle."

"That might not fly with them, Paige. These are finance executives. They're probably expecting charts."

"Charts of what?"

"You know what I mean. Hard data."

"Okay, make a pie chart. Knock yourself out," Paige grinned. "I'm going to practice my jazz hands."

At twenty minutes past one, a smiling Paige and a drenched-with-nervous-sweat-Sophie were let inside a room where six executives sat around a boardroom table.

"USB?" the woman who'd ushered them inside said, waving at the large screen at the end of the table. "For your presentation?" she added when Sophie stared at her dumbly. Her nerves were threatening to engulf her completely. Paige took the USB from Sophie's sweaty clutch and handed it to the assistant with a smile.

"Let's get started, shall we?" Josh said with a nod and a wink for Sophie.

Sophie pushed down the surge of nausea and offered him a weak smile in return as Paige stepped forward and said. "Good afternoon, gentlemen."

THEY NAILED THE presentation.

The executive team, looking bored at first, had perked up at the mention of narcissistic personality disorder, and looked positively enthralled when Paige explained how cases such as this could have a flow-on effect on productivity and ultimately profit.

And Sophie had been right about the pie charts, they'd loved those.

They left the executives in the room with Josh to discuss 'next steps' and made their way to the elevator bay trying to keep their excited whispering to a minimum.

"Josh has already texted to suggest we celebrate. He'll be out of that meeting in twenty minutes, he thinks. Should we go?"

Sophie was feeling a lot better and quite fancied the idea of going for drinks, even if it was with Josh. "We probably should. Let's put our laptops and stuff in my car."

But when the elevator dinged at the third floor and Sophie went to get out, Paige stayed where she was, engrossed in a text that had just come in.

Sophie held open the door. "Paige?"

"Listen, I've got to run a quick errand, but I'll be back, okay?"

"Where on earth are you going?"

"I'll explain later. Text me your location and I'll meet you there." Paige pressed the button for ground floor.


SOPHIE WAS HALFWAY through a glass of red wine and feeling pretty good, but where on earth was Paige? She'd texted her fifteen minutes ago to tell her she and Josh were at Vivace in Fort Street, and gotten an *OK* in return, but Paige still hadn't shown up. Josh was thrilled it was just the two of them, Sophie could tell, and he kept inching his chair closer to hers when he thought she wasn't looking. Sophie pulled out her phone again and gave Josh a nervous smile. A cosy drink without Paige was not a good idea.

The waitress appeared at their table. "Something to nibble on?"

Josh's face contorted and Sophie could tell he was controlling the urge to make a suggestive joke. At least he was controlling it, Sophie thought, relaxing a little more. Maybe she'd been worrying about nothing.

"Absolutely," Josh said, proceeding to order without waiting for Sophie's input.

As Josh selected items from the tapas menu, she studied him. Depending on how he angled his face, he could look quite handsome—when his head was down and tilted to the side a bit so he was showing off his cheekbones—but when he lifted his head, his chin disappeared and he was all nose and eyebrows, bordering on unattractive. Sophie had read once George Clooney had been advised by some astute woman—before he got famous—that his success would depend on how he held his head. He had a particular angle that worked for him, and anything else would resign him to forever be one of the hopeful but unknown masses. Sophie had gone back and watched some old episodes of ER and noticed that indeed, wherever possible, he kept his head angled down, so he could look up with those big soulful eyes. As she watched Josh hand the menu back to the waitress but continue to keep his head angled in that downward position, Sophie suspected Josh might be all too aware of the importance of angles.

PAIGE BOUNDED UP the stairs to S &S Investigations.

The text had been from Eddie. He was worried because Hazel had missed an appointment and he didn't know where she was. *Was Paige at the office?* he asked. *Could she check her office and the nearby streets?*

When Paige got to the top of the stairs she could see keys hanging out of Hazel's door and went straight inside. It took less than a minute to determine that Hazel was not there. As threads of unease turned into flutters of panic, Paige went to Hazel's desk and rummaged through each of the drawers. She wasn't sure what she was achieving by violating Hazel's privacy like this, but she had to do something, and detectives in the movies often found useful clues by looking through desk drawers. Unfortunately, there was nothing of interest in Hazel's. On the desk were two framed photos that Paige hadn't spotted during her previous visits: an old-looking family photo with two teenage girls—one of them was clearly Hazel and the other looked like her sister—and then a more recent photo of Hazel with a man who was probably the now deceased husband, John. But this didn't tell Paige anything she didn't already know.

As she moved away from the photos she spotted a notepad sitting on the desk by the computer. She grabbed a pencil from the pen holder and scribbled on the top sheet. If this was an episode of Murder She Wrote, she'd soon be able to make out an important phone number or an address by the indents on the paper. A minute later she reviewed the mass of grey scribbles on the notepad and threw it down on the desk with frustration.

She looked around the room again, this time seeing the filing cabinet in the corner. But it was locked. "Damn," she hissed, planting her hands on her hips. As the cold metal of the keys dug into her hand, Paige remembered she had Hazel's keys. She found the small key for the filing cabinet straight away.

The top two drawers were dedicated to client files. In the third, bottom drawer, Hazel kept her important business paperwork, such as tax returns and paid invoices, various accounts with suppliers and providers; but also a file labelled *Personal.* Inside was Hazel's last will and testament. Paige flicked through it, noting Hazel was leaving her entire estate to a charity for children, then found something of particular relevance. An invoice for a medical consultation at a doctor's clinic in Dunedin.

"Aha!" Paige cried, clutching the paper. Hazel had had a relatively recent appointment with Doctor Fletcher. Just before she returned to Auckland, it seemed. And there was an address. This wouldn't explain where Hazel was right now, but it seemed important.

Still holding the invoice, Paige locked the door behind her and put Hazel's keys inside her bag as she walked around the landing toward the top of the stairs. There, she paused. The door to 2B was dark and when she stepped closer it was quiet, but that weird interaction she'd had with Hazel a while back, when Hazel had said something about her sister and gone inside, popped into Paige's mind. The door was locked, so it was unlikely Hazel was in there, but it was still worth a look. She retrieved Hazel's keys from her bag and tried one after the other until she found the one that slid into 2B.

Paige walked through the completely empty first office then carried on through the door to the right where there was a second, smaller office. It too, seemed empty at first, until she spotted a white cord in the darkness of the corner. When she went over there, she saw that it was a phone charger.

What on earth was a phone charger doing in here?

A SERIES OF tapas plates were delivered to the table in a succession of deliciousness, and even though Paige had now texted to say she couldn't come after all, Sophie found that she wasn't particularly concerned. Josh wasn't so bad, really. He was just overly keen and a bit full of his own importance.

Josh reached his hand across the table and made a sympathetic noise. "You seem distracted. Is there anything you want to talk about? Get off your chest?"

"I do?" Sophie retracted her hand, but slowly, so she didn't seem rude, and considered the question. Even with a red wine glow, the business of Roman and Anya was still bothering her, but she couldn't very well talk about that. She could, however, ask Josh what he thought about Kate and Harry.

"Kate, being found dead in her apartment. It's kind of shocking."

Josh nodded, his forehead creasing in concern. "Yeah. Makes you think, doesn't it. At any moment, your time could be up. Every day is precious and it could be your last. We have to live life to the fullest, you know?" Josh adopted a wise and knowing smile, as if a million other people hadn't already said something like this before.

"Yeah." Sophie nodded. "I'm also kind of worried about Harry."

"Harry?" Josh had gone a little pale.

"Yes, he's a payroll clerk?"

"Hey, let's take a selfie. It's such a nice evening," Josh said abruptly.

"I don't know..."

But Josh had already pulled out his phone and scooched over to Sophie. "Here we go." Josh positioned the camera and Sophie offered an unenthusiastic smile.

"There," Josh said, posting it on social media. "All done." He beamed as if he'd done Sophie a favour. "Hey. Why the sad face?" Josh attempted a jovial tone.

"It's silly, I know, but I can't stop worrying about Harry."

Josh swallowed. "Why?"

"He's off sick, but I don't know... I think it might be more than that."

"Nah, he's just got the flu." Josh took a nervous sip of beer.

Sophie eyed Josh, her head clearing a little as she focused her attention. She didn't think Josh was lying, exactly. But something was up. He knew something about Harry, she was sure of it.

"Josh, is Harry's absence from work to do with sickness or not?"

"How would I know? He's a junior pleb." Josh increased the volume of his voice.

Sophie picked up her water and took a long pull, eyeing Josh over the glass.

"Hey... hey. Let's not talk shop. Let's enjoy our evening."

Sophie let the moment hang for a beat before she said, "I think maybe it's time to go."

When Josh said eagerly, "I'll get the bill," her stomach plummeted because it was obvious he thought she meant leave here and go somewhere else together. Like his apartment. He'd already gone on about the super cool bachelor pad he owned on Parnell Rise. Before Sophie could correct him, Josh was up and halfway across the room. How was she going to fend off his advances?

Outside, as they strolled down to Quay Street, she took a rallying breath and said, "Listen, Josh, I've got to get home. Thanks for dinner and drinks, and everything, but I'm really tired so I'm going to jump into a cab."

"Oh, come on, Sophie. We've had such a nice night." Josh stepped closer and wrapped his arms around her, effectively pinning her arms to her side. "Let's not end it just yet."

Sophie tried to wriggle away. "We have, thank you, but I've really got to go."

"Mmmm, what was that?" Josh said, pulling her even closer so his entire body was pressed against hers, and leaning down as if to kiss her.

"No!" She broke free from his grip. "Sorry, Josh, but no."

"Come on." Josh wrapped his arms around her torso and pulled the now obviously struggling Sophie against him. Sophie placed both hands against his chest and pushed back as hard as she could.

"Josh! I said, no."

He staggered back, his eyes glinting with anger. "After all I've done for you? You could be a little grateful." His voice was hard.

"I am, but that doesn't mean I'm going to…" Sophie trailed off, watching as Josh's eyes turn icy. "We work together. I'm essentially your employee."

"Not any anymore you aren't." He threw the words at her.

"What?"

"Hiring you was a mistake. Utter amateurs. Don't worry, I'll make sure everyone knows all about it. Just you wait."

"Josh, please."

"No, too late. You've ruined it," Josh hissed. "Cock tease," he added under his breath.

Sophie recoiled and lurched to the side of the street. A taxi was approaching so she thrust out a hand to flag it down.

"Pt Chev, please," she said to the driver. "Quickly," she added getting in as Josh stepped up to the window. His face contorted into an ugly expression. All the windows were up so she couldn't make out what Josh called out after the departing taxi, but she got the gist.

Sophie leaned against the seat in a state of shock. In the space of a couple of minutes, everything had turned into a disaster.

# 14

It was midday before Sophie could bring herself to get out of bed. She would have happily stayed there all day, but this was getting to be a bit of a habit. Plus, she had to tell Paige what had happened and she couldn't justify doing that by text. Or even over the phone. No, this was a face to face conversation. With a weary sigh Sophie texted Paige and told her to meet at S & S at two o'clock. They hadn't scheduled any interviews for today, in case they needed to make changes after the presentation, and to give the employees a bit more time after learning about Kate.

Alone in the flat, Sophie took her time in the shower, washing her hair twice as she played the memory of Josh, his face contorting with malice as he said those horrible things, over and over in her head. Why had she stayed with him when she found out Paige wasn't coming? She'd known Josh wouldn't take rejection well, but she didn't expect him to turn quite that nasty. And they were fired, which was bad enough, but would there be worse repercussions? Josh clearly had a vindictive side, and after their successful presentation how would he explain firing them to the executives without making something up?

Everything was a mess and the whole thing was exhausting.

At half past one, dressed in her comfort outfit of leggings, a singlet and a large check shirt she could wrap around her waist, Sophie trudged up to the S & S office.

Waiting outside the door was a surprise.

Polly Dixon.


LEO OPENED THE envelope Alice had handed him and looked up, a line of confusion creasing his brow. "This is too much. The money in here is way too much."

"Don't worry," Alice hushed him. "It's fine. You've worked hard in the garden, you've done so much to help me. I know things are a bit tight for you at the moment. And I don't want you to be beholden to that Barrett any more. He sounds dreadful. Now you have enough to pay him back."

Leo had done a fair amount of complaining about Barrett over the past few days, and may have exaggerated a little, so he felt a bit bad, but not really. Barrett had been a complete tool about the whole thing, and he suspected Alice wouldn't be hassling him every five seconds for the return of money she didn't need.

"I'll pay you back. I promise."

"No rush." Alice smiled and Leo smiled back.

The moment hung, awkwardness creeping in.

While both of them wanted to return to the romantic atmosphere of the other afternoon, neither of them wanted to do so immediately after money had exchanged hands. So, Leo gave her a peck on the cheek and said he'd see her tomorrow.

Twenty minutes later he parked his car and walked down the driveway of his parent's house to his studio unit. There was no need to duck this time because the parents weren't home.

Even from twenty feet away he could see Emmitt's angry silhouette in the window. Leo groaned. It was hard to get used to owning a permanent pet, especially in his current distracted state.

"Hey, buddy," Leo said, opening the door. Inside, the acrid smell of cat urine greeted him. Emmitt continued to sit on the window sill, eyeing Leo with defiance.

"Ah, nuts," Leo said, his gaze moving from the cleaning supplies cupboard under the sink, to Emmitt, wondering which he should deal with first. Finally, he went over to Emmitt and gave his head a good scratch. "I forgot to feed you this morning, didn't I? Sorry, buddy, my head is somewhere else at the moment. Are you hungry?"

"Meow," Emmitt said indignantly. Indeed, he was.

POLLY SAT ACROSS from Sophie on one of the visitor chairs under the window with both knees drawn up to her chest, pulling at the hem of her long floral skirt.

"You're sure you don't want coffee?" Sophie asked.

Polly shook her head, then lifted her gaze to meet Sophie's. "I came to say thank you." Polly swallowed and cleared her throat. "Sorry, this is still a little difficult to talk about."

Sophie nodded.

A couple of months ago Polly had gone missing, and despite her parents not agreeing to hire S & S, Paige had insisted they find her anyway, hopeful that it would turn into a real, paying, case—which indeed it had. Sophie and Paige had found Polly and revealed the kidnapping culprit to be her father. He'd ferreted Polly away to an unused bach in the Coromandel in order to keep his activist daughter from spilling the beans about the dodgy business deal he was brokering. Even though he'd kept her sedated, no harm had come to Polly, and the business deal had not been illegal, so in the end the matter had been dropped. The Dixon family were attending family counselling, however, which seemed to Sophie like a necessary, if perhaps insufficient, step to repair the damage that had been done.

"Mum told me she didn't even properly hire you until after you'd found me. And I heard you, explaining it all, at the end. You were," Polly looked down at her hands, "amazing." She fiddled with the cuff of her sleeve. "You've made me want to know stuff. To be able to do what you do. Like, I want to study psychology. Or physiological systems, or criminology… or something."

Hearing this, in the face of everything that had happened, was making Sophie dangerously emotional, on the precipice of bursting into tears even, but she managed to control herself and her facial muscles before responding.

"Polly, that's great. But you're not giving up your activist work, are you? I was impressed by you too. Your commitment and selflessness."

Sophie was starting to feel rather grown-up.

"I'll keep doing that, for sure, but I'm definitely going to spend more time at uni."

Sophie beamed. "Good on you."

"And I was wondering..." Polly was now pulling at the thread on her jumper and Sophie was resisting the urge to get the scissors from the drawer and cut it off. "Would you consider being, like, my mentor? For like, my university studies... and stuff?"

Sophie was speechless. And tears were threatening, *again*. She had to take a moment, looking down at her hands on her lap, before attempting to speak.

In her silence, Polly continued. "Mum is great, and I'm happy that she's been a stay-at-home Mum, but I don't think it's been that exciting for her, you know? And she doesn't want that for me.

And now I kind of get it, you know. After seeing you, and..." Polly looked up and off to the side, trying to remember the name.

"Paige."

Polly nodded. "I want to be like you. I want to be able to do what you can do."

"Of course I'll be your mentor, Polly." Sophie beamed.

Ten minutes later, Polly had left but Sophie was still sitting at her desk, somewhat stunned. Someone wanted *her* to mentor them. Sophie had never done that before, but she knew what it meant, at least in an academic setting. A mentor was person, usually older, who had been through the system already and could show them the ropes, provide advice, and generally be a more knowledgeable support person. Sophie's lip wobbled dramatically and she nearly succumbed to the moment, but she shook her head and pushed back her shoulders and took a deep breath.

She was Polly's mentor.

That *meant* something.

Her phone beeped. It was message from Paige.

*Can't meet today sorry.*

Sophie bit her lip. Paige had bailed on her without much explanation last night, and now this?

*Why not?*

*In Dunedin. Talk later.*

"Dunedin?" Sophie exclaimed out loud. "Dunedin???"

What was Paige doing in the South Island? Sophie chewed on the inside of her cheek. Whatever it was, it was likely to be some self-involved endeavour. That was for sure. And after everything that had happened with Josh, this felt like a total abandonment.

She picked up her phone again, then set it down. What should she do? She had that awful Josh situation to deal with but she couldn't do it on her own, she just couldn't. And that was precisely where Paige shone. Confrontations. She would wait until Paige was back to deal with that issue, she decided, but in the meantime, she had to do *something*. Sophie was a mentor now, so she had to step up and be mentor-worthy material. She picked up her phone again. She was going to find out what was going on with Harry.

She called Leo. "What are you doing right now?"

Blushing even though no one could see him, Leo said. "Nothing."

"Come to the office. I need you."

Sophie hung up and started pacing the office. She was now fairly certain that Harry's absence was not to do with the flu. Yes, it may be due to drug use, but why did Josh act so strangely when she'd asked him? Combined with the burning anger she'd seen in Josh's eyes, she was now wondering what Josh was capable of, and whether Harry might be in some serious trouble indeed.

Leo arrived at S & S with a rosy glow to his cheeks and looking rather pleased with himself. Sophie made a mental note to ask him about that later, then put him to work locating Harry's home address.

Ten minutes later he cleared his throat. "I've found his apartment building. And I didn't even need to hack anything." Despite this being his main 'thing' up until a few months ago, Leo found the idea of sneaking around people's personal accounts rather distasteful. He was used to hacking into faceless corporations, and mostly just for the hell of it. All in all, Leo was not cut out for a hacker's life.

"He's active on Instagram and he posts stuff about where he eats and goes, and he's also got photos from inside his apartment," Leo continued. "It's somewhere on K' Road. It's not an address but I know the building. Although," Leo frowned as he scrolled, "he hasn't posted in the past week. It's possible he's moved, I guess."

"We'll try there first, and if not, can you like, track him by his mobile phone or something?"

Leo had done this when they were trying to find Polly.

"Do you have his number?"

"Rats. No. I could probably get it off Denise, but I'm not sure I can access the building anymore," Sophie said miserably.


THE RECEPTIONIST AT the Dunedin medical centre was getting a headache.

"Well?" Paige said.

"You must realise I can't tell you anything about a patient."

Paige sighed and narrowed her eyes. She was about to continue her assault when a woman holding a medical file emerged from the hall.

"Doctor Fletcher?" Paige called out to the woman who stopped, startled, then nodded.

The receptionist briefly considered stopping this pushy little madam from bothering the doctor, but then decided she didn't have the strength.

Paige strode over. "Dr Garnet," she began, holding out her hand, hoping to give the impression she was also a medical doctor, a colleague. "Your patient, Hazel Berryman, is missing. She's been experiencing strange symptoms. Please, will you talk to me?"

As Dr Fletcher held out her hand to shake Paige's, her eyebrows lifted. "I'm surprised to hear that. Yes, come through."

The conversation started off well. The doctor informed Paige that Hazel had been to see her for a physical, something she did once a year to keep an eye on things, and this had revealed a clean bill of health. But once she realised Paige was not in fact a 'real doctor' and that it was therefore completely inappropriate to discuss a Hazel's medical situation with her, she closed down Hazel's medical record with an angry sigh, and clamped up.

But Paige persisted, and after another five minutes the doctor, like the receptionist, was desperate to be rid of Paige.

"Listen, all I can tell you, is what you are saying is completely inconsistent with what I observed of Hazel. And I hope you find her, I do, but I can't talk about, or release, her medical records. Hazel herself, her new doctor, or her power of attorney are the only ones who can request her records."

As Paige left, she wondered whether Eddie had thought to try to get power of attorney. She couldn't imagine it would be the sort of thing you could do very easily, surely. It would take a bit of time, and from what Eddie had told her, Hazel hadn't been showing symptoms for all that long. It seemed unlikely, but it was worth checking. She needed to talk to Eddie anyway. She hadn't spoken to him since she'd confirmed with him that Hazel wasn't at the office. She hadn't even told him she was coming down here. She thought Eddie might tell her to back off, that she was overstepping the mark. Better to take action now and apologise later, was Paige's Go-To approach. Still, she should find out if there was any news about Hazel. She pulled out her phone and called Eddie, but he wasn't picking up. Perhaps that was a good sign. Perhaps that meant Hazel was back and safe and so he didn't need to stay by his phone.

SOPHIE AND LEO had located Harry's building and determined which floor they thought he lived on. And they didn't even need to figure out a way to be buzzed in, because some clueless person had propped open the front door with a battered phonebook.

They ascended the grotty stairs to the second floor. Outside the apartment they guessed Harry lived in—based on photograph angles—Sophie nodded to Leo, then knocked on the door. Silence. Sophie knocked again. No answer. Sophie raised her shoulders in a helpless gesture and Leo, all of sudden caught up by the drama of it all, surged forward and thrust himself against the door.

"Ow!" he bellowed, rubbing his shoulder.

Sophie watched Leo with wide eyes.

"I just thought..." Leo shook his head and shot a sulky look at the unyielding door. How cool would that have been, if it had given way and they'd found Harry tied up inside or something.

"Now what?" Sophie said, biting the inside of her lip.

Leo was still staring at the door, thinking this place reminded him of his flat when he was a university student. He, like Harry, had lived alone in a studio apartment, and the second time he forgot his keys he'd hidden a spare one near the door. He didn't have anything worth stealing, and the hassle of realising you couldn't get into your apartment at two a.m. on a Wednesday was worse than someone relieving you of your crappy belongings.

"I bet he's hidden a key around here somewhere," Leo said. There was a grubby welcome mat outside Harry's neighbour's door, so while Leo ran his hands along the edges of the door frame, Sophie checked there. They both found nothing. Leo walked a few feet back toward the top of the stairs and noticed a pipe running up the wall. He moved closer, examining the surrounding area, until he saw it. A strip of clear plastic Sellotape. He felt around the back of the pipe until his hand brushed against the cold but familiar shape of a key. "Aha!" Leo detached it and held it up for Sophie to see.

"You legend, Leo," Sophie said, beaming at him. "How'd you know to look there?"

"I did the same thing when I lived in a place like this." Leo inserted the key, glanced to his left and right, as if to check that Harry's neighbours weren't watching, and opened the door. Sophie thought that if Harry's neighbours were home and the kind of people who cared about Harry's place getting burgled, they probably would have made an appearance when Leo was trying to break down the door.

The stale stench of weed hung like a cloud, almost visible, inside Harry's studio apartment. His flat was a reflection of his mental and emotional state, Sophie thought as she stepped over a pizza box on her way to the living room area of the studio apartment. She might be getting a contact high just from being in here.

It took all of three seconds to determine Harry wasn't home—hiding in a corner or under the bed. What Sophie did find, next to a hip-height bundle of clothes that masked the presence of a tiny dining table, was an iPad. She immediately turned it on and was confronted by a passcode.

"No worries," Leo said, taking the iPad from her. He pressed the button at the bottom, then said "John Cena" out loud. The iPad came to life as it complied with his verbal request for a search on the famous wrestler. A few short taps and swipes later, Leo had opened the iPad. "Let's look at his search engine."

"That was ridiculously easy," Sophie said, her mind racing to think what someone would find on her recent searches if they hacked in like this. A blush blossomed on her cheeks. She must remember to select the option to clear search history on exit.

"I think he might be in Hamilton," Leo said after a second. "Look. Intercity bus schedules and cheap motels in Hamilton."

"Someone who is just off sick doesn't go to Hamilton, do they," Sophie said.

"Yeah, but someone pulling a sicky because they want to go to watch Speedway or something does."

"Fine, okay. But if you take this in consideration with all Harry's other behaviour and the way Josh was acting, I don't think he's just wagging work."

"So why is he there? Visiting a friend?"

Sophie chewed on the inside of her lip as she concentrated. Harry and Kate were both payroll clerks. Harry had seemed increasingly stressed out, paranoid even, and then he went to Kate's house even though he knew she was on leave.

"It's got to be something to do with payroll. And he seems to be running away. But from what?" Sophie continued to chew the inside of her lip. She couldn't stop thinking about Harry's grey anxious face. For some reason she felt responsible for that twitchy man-boy. Now that she knew he was using cannabis to calm himself down—he had to be, the way this place smelt—she thought his mental state might be rather fragile indeed.

"Leo, we have to find him. How do we figure out his location in Hamilton?"

"He's at Motel Six in Abbortsford Street," Leo said pointing at the iPad. "It's right there."

"Awesome. Okay... Let's go." Sophie strode toward the door.

Leo hesitated.

Sophie turned back. "What's wrong?"

Leo's shift at the DVD rental place started in an hour. "Um..."

"Oh, right. You're probably busy... I didn't even think," Sophie grimaced, "I could go on my own," she added unconvincingly.

Leo thought about going on an exciting adventure with Sophie to save this Harry person, and then he thought about sitting behind the counter at the store, where he'd probably to have to explain the plot of every single movie to one indecisive person who would end up going home to stream something illegally anyway, then suddenly having five people all clamouring for his attention and being kind of rude about it. Not to mention Barrett knew he was working tonight so he'd probably pop by and pretend he hadn't been acting like an utter knob about the money he'd lent Leo.

"Nope, nothing I can't get out of. Let's go."


THE CARPARK AT Motel Six had only three cars, but they knew Harry had come by bus, so that was no help. The bored-looking person sitting in reception had glanced at them as they cruised in and parked, but had remained sitting in the cubicle, clearly not paid enough to get up and find out what they were doing there.

Sophie and Leo were now sitting in Sophie's Volkswagen Jetta, unsure what to do next except wait for some sign of Harry.

"Sorry about your car, again," Leo said awkwardly.

"Yeah, uh, no worries," Sophie said, although she'd only recently forgiven Leo for smashing into her beloved Jetta during his pet-napping escapades. The first time Leo had gotten into this car he'd said, shame-faced, "I'll pay you for the damages," but he'd then forgotten all about it. Until he got into the car this afternoon that is, and he'd realised that any payment they offered for his recent work would have to be refused, at least until he'd paid off that debt.

"So," Sophie said, to change the subject. "Why have you been looking so cheerful lately? Got a new lady?"

Sophie had been joking, but when she saw the shade of red Leo turned, she knew she was right on the money.

"Oh my god, you're seeing someone? Who? Where did you meet them?" Sophie felt a pang of jealousy, but managed to cover it up.

"Oh, uh," Leo looked down.

"Leo?" Sophie prompted.

"Through you two. Or, I guess, Paige."

Sophie frowned. Who on earth could Leo be referring to?

"She got me a job working for her mother, in the garden."

Sophie nodded, already aware of this.

"And, uh, she's a lovely woman," Leo finished with a smile.

"Mrs Garnet?" Sophie's voice rose a couple of octaves.

"Do you think it's weird?" Leo suddenly looked stricken.

"Oh, uh..." Sort of, Sophie thought. But she couldn't ruin it for him. Leo was obviously thrilled. "No, but does Paige know?" Sophie knew that Paige couldn't possibly be aware of this. She wouldn't have heard the end of it otherwise.

"Not yet. But we're going to tell her. When the time is right," Leo said earnestly.

Sophie resisted the urge to sarcastically wish Leo good luck and said instead, "You and Alice Garnet, huh?"

Leo nodded. "She's so great," he said, his smile widening again.

"Well, good for you," Sophie said, not quite sure what Leo saw in Alice, except for her resemblance to Paige, of course.

As Sophie turned back to look out the window, it occurred to her than even Paige's mother was now hooked up. Why did everyone else get to find love except her?

"What if he never comes out of his room?" Leo said after a while.

"I was just thinking that," Sophie said. "So, do we go room to room? Knock on each door?"

"Maybe?" Leo shrugged.

"Hey, what's your sense of smell like?"

"Huh?"

"Harry's flat smelled like the morning after a Snoop Dog party. I think he's smoking a lot to help with whatever he's stressing about. It's probably making him super paranoid as well but..."

"You think we should walk around and sniff the rooms?"

Sophie raised her shoulders. "You got a better idea?"

They took one end of the u-shaped block of units each. Five minutes later, Leo waved at Sophie frantically from the far side. Sophie raced over. "Was I right?"

"I don't know if it's Harry, but someone has definitely been smoking up in there."

Here goes nothing, Sophie thought, and knocked on the door. There was a startled yelp, then a thump. "Harry?" Sophie called through the door. "Is that you? It's Sophie...We met the other day at work. I just want to talk to you. Please. I, uh," Sophie took a gamble, "I know you're in trouble and I can help."

Several tense seconds passed as Sophie and Leo waited for Harry to decide whether to let them in. Then, with a resigned sigh and the click of a lock, the door opened. Harry's face was pale and there were bags under his eyes.

"Thanks," Sophie said, stepping past him as he held open the door wide enough for them to come in.

"Heya, Harry," Leo said brightly.

Sophie looked around the messy, weed-infused space—Harry had made himself at home—and said, "Shall we go somewhere to talk?"

Harry's eyes shifted nervously from Sophie to Leo. "Is it safe?"

Sophie and Leo exchanged a glance. "We'll go somewhere no-one can hear us, okay?" Sophie said.

Ten minutes later, they were set up in a corner table at Helm Bar & Kitchen. It wasn't a particularly quiet bar, but they were able to find a table without any neighbours. After sitting down, both Leo and Sophie realised they were now rather hungry, so they ordered a selection of fried food for the table and three beers. Sophie didn't usually drink beer, but it seemed appropriate. She was in Hamilton, after all. A few minutes later they were sipping at lagers and tucking into an order of chips and mini spring rolls. At least, Sophie and Leo were; Harry was staring into his beer, his shoulders hunched over as if this might make him invisible. When he finally looked up, his still nervous eyes skittered across Sophie's face, then flicked to Leo.

"Is he your muscle?" he said.

Leo brightened as he looked down at his arms and flexed his bicep. He could see the muscle moving under his skin. Leo beamed. He was certainly in the best shape of his life, there was no doubt about that. His diet and all that gardening had paid off.

"No, he's a colleague."

"Humph." Harry was clawing at the already distressed hangnail on his thumb.

Sophie put out a gentle hand to stop him before he drew blood. "I was hired to do psychometric testing. Whatever else is going on... I'm not here to catch you out. I'm here to help. You can trust me."

Harry looked into his beer.

"You're obviously worried. Something is bothering you... Or someone?"

Harry's brows creased into a frown and he continued looking down.

"We're not cops, Harry."

All of a sudden, Harry seemed to give up. "Fine." His shoulders dropped a couple of inches and he sighed with resignation. "I don't know what to do anymore anyway. I can't just stay here, can I?" Harry leaned forward, nearly knocking his beer over, took a breath, and told them. He let it all out. Ten minutes later, he abruptly stopped talking and started shovelling chips into his mouth. Once he'd finished them off, he took a big gulp of beer and sat back. "Now what?"

Sophie nodded slowly, still trying to process what he'd told her.

"I... I'm on it. Don't worry. I'll, uh... sort it. And thank you. You've done the right thing."

Harry nodded then stood abruptly. "Excuse me," he said, lurching off to the back of the restaurant toward the toilets. Harry fumbled at the buttons on his jeans as he pushed open the door.

Leo watched Harry stagger away, then turned back to Sophie.

"So, do we call the cops?"

"We don't have any proof. We have Harry's suspicions and his opinion about who is responsible."

"We should probably still tell them."

"The thing is though, Leo, I signed a confidentiality agreement." This had occurred to Sophie while Harry was explaining what he thought was going on.

"It says I can't discuss anything I learn about the employees."

"Even if it's illegal?"

"But what if Harry's wrong? What if they sue me?"

Leo shrugged helplessly.

BACK IN AUCKLAND, at one of the downtown bars that turns into more of a club when work drinks turn into more serious drinking—when ties have been loosened or removed, and women have been to the bathroom to drunkenly let out their hair and apply much fiercer make-up—Josh leaned against the bar and surveyed the room.

Spite coursed through him, brimming up to the surface, turning his face ugly. He'd had a series of unpleasant meetings over the last two days, but Sophie's rejection was still eating away at him.

After all he'd done for her.

It burned in his chest.

He felt small and unimportant, but he wasn't, dammit. How dare she make him feel like that? And how was he going to rid himself of this toxic sentiment? He downed the rest of his drink and slammed the glass on the counter. The bartender eyed him warily.

Josh cast his eyes around the room again, searching for familiar faces. He'd posted a generic invitation on social media to see who was out tonight, needing a partner in crime, someone to drown his sorrows with or at least distract him, but no one had responded so far. The crowd was a mix of those who'd been here for a while, looking a little worse for wear, as well as much shinier people who'd obviously arrived more recently.

Then he saw her. Walking right toward him.

"Oh, wow."

Hannah took a seat at the bar and smiled at Josh as she adjusted her hair.

"You look like... Can I buy you a drink?"

Josh was not a shy individual, but he surprised even himself with this abrupt confidence. Then again, he was on his third drink and he'd gone straight to the top shelf tonight.

"Vodka soda," Hannah said. "You must know Sophie?"

Josh gritted his teeth as the memory of his attempt to kiss her flared unpleasantly in his mind. "A little. Through work."

Hannah tilted her head. "You guys didn't date or anything?"

Josh considered this for a moment then said, "We had dinner and she wanted more, but I said we shouldn't. Not while we're working together."

"Huh," Hannah said, wrapping the end of her hair around her index finger, fluttering her eyelashes and pushing her lips out into a fuller pout. Josh stared at her, mesmerized. She was so like Sophie, but she had an edge to her, and she was sexy as hell. Sexier than Sophie, that's for sure.

"Let's get you that drink then, shall we?" He smiled and waved at the bartender.

# 15

Technically they were fired, but Sophie had to do something. She'd promised Harry, after all, and it was possible that Kate had discovered the same thing.

And look what had happened to her.

It was nearly ten p.m. by the time she and Leo got back into town, but she had to sort this out now.

Sophie pulled up outside the house on Western Springs Road and turned to Leo. "Hey, can you stay in the car? This will probably go better with just me there."

Leo looked a little put out but said, "Sure."

Sophie knocked on the door of the house above Kate's unit. It took another knock and an obvious peering-through-the-curtains before someone answered.

"Hi, sorry to call around so late, but it's important," Sophie said. "Are you Chloe?"

She nodded.

"I wondered if you had a second. I want to ask you about Kate."

Chloe stared at Sophie wide-eyed for a moment, then opened the door to let her inside. Sophie took a seat in the living room while Chloe made them each a cup of tea. As soon as Chloe had handed Sophie her mug and sat down, her lower lip started to tremble.

"It was so awful." She shook her head. "I was there when the landlord opened the door... and... the smell." She looked down and gathered herself before speaking again. "I stayed outside at first, but after the police and ambulance had gone, I went back in. I don't know why, really. It still didn't seem real."

Sophie nodded encouragingly.

Chloe spent five minutes talking in a rambling way about Kate. They hadn't known each other particularly well, but enough to chitchat at the letterbox. Finally, she blew her nose and said, "Do you know what was kind of weird? It looked like she'd packed this book that she'd already read."

"Maybe she wanted to re-read it?"

"But she hadn't liked it. She told me because I was thinking about borrowing it. She said it was a chore to get through. She was going to throw it out."

"Hmm," Sophie said. "Do you remember seeing any visitors at Kate's place recently? I mean, people you maybe hadn't seen visit her before?"

Chloe reddened. "I mean, it's not as if I spend all my time watching out the window, but my bedroom is at the front and when someone walks by, I notice."

"So, she did?"

"I can't remember when it was exactly, but I remember because they looked so out of place, you know?

Sophie pulled out her phone and spent a few moments searching and scrolling until she found a photo. She held it up for Chloe.

Chloe nodded. "That's the one."

THE NEXT MORNING, Sophie picked Leo up from his place in Mt Eden and they drove downtown. She paid through the nose for a parking spot and then they found a coffee shop so they could fine-tune the hazy plan that had come to Sophie in the early hours of the morning. A little over an hour later they sucked back the last of their coffee, attempted a rallying handshake, and crossed the road to enter the lobby of the building.

"Hi there," she said brightly to the security guard, trying to look confident as she held her access card up to the reader on the turnstiles. She held her breath for the micro-second it took to turn green then exhaled with relief. Josh couldn't have told anyone she was fired yet.

Now to get Leo in.

She gave the guard what she hoped was a charming and not at all suspicious smile and gestured at Leo, still waiting on the other side. "I have the new IT guy to take up to Denise in HR. He hasn't got his access card yet. Can you let him through?"

Leo looked at the guard with a hopeful smile, who gave him a cursory glance—Leo looked about as dangerous as a golden retriever—and turned back to beam at Sophie.

"Sure, love. Here you go." He opened the door for Leo.

"Thank you."

Sophie clutched excitedly at Leo as they headed toward the elevator bay. They were in.

On the eighth floor, they exited the elevator and went to hover in the little nook to the left near the water cooler.

"Okay, Leo, make the call and say there's a package downstairs that has to be signed for. Be insistent. From here you can see when it's safe to go into the office."

Leo nodded and got out his phone.

"Remember, you're only going to have a few minutes. Here's the bank account you're looking for." Sophie shoved a piece of paper into his hand. "Call me if you run into any issues, otherwise I'll meet you back here in five minutes."

Outside Josh's office, Sophie wiped sweaty palms on her skirt, threw back her shoulders and inhaled deeply. She had to do this, no matter how much dread was barrelling through her body, making her stomach contract unpleasantly. For a second she considered bolting for the bathroom, but then shook her head. No, she thought. Just do it. Go in there and tell him.

According to Harry, the only thing Josh was guilty of—apart from being a creep—was buying drugs from Harry. So, Sophie was here to try to get him back on side. If Josh was the one to reveal the scam and save the day, then maybe he wouldn't be so mad at Sophie, and maybe he wouldn't follow through on his threat to damn S & S Investigations publicly.

Sophie hovered at Josh's office door, eyeing Josh. He was at his desk, sipping slowly from a venti-sized coffee, staring at his phone. His eyes were bloodshot and he'd done a terrible job of shaving this morning. Sophie thought she'd probably be able to smell alcohol vapours once she got inside.

Having to deal with a hung-over Josh was not ideal. But she had to do this.

JOSH DIDN'T HEAR the first knock, but at the second he looked up and saw Sophie.

"What the hell are you doing here?" Josh threw the words at her. "I fired you, remember?"

"I'm sorry, Josh. About, uh, dinner, but we work together, so…"

"Whatever." Josh waved his hand to dismiss her. "I've already moved on." He took another sip of coffee. He couldn't quite remember what happened at the end of the night, and even though he'd woken up alone, without his wallet—he must have left it in the Uber so he'd call later and sort that out—he was sure the evening had gone well and he'd even managed to kiss Hannah. He had her number in his phone, after all, saved with a photo of her smiling seductively. He'd text her later to see if she was as hungover as he was, and what she was doing this weekend. He had a feeling that Hannah was going to be a lot of fun. The question was, when should he tell Sophie?

"You have? Oh, good." Sophie looked relieved "Listen, I'm here because I have something important to tell you. It's about payroll."

Josh squinted at Sophie as his head continued to pound. The three Neurofen he'd taken half an hour ago weren't working yet and he was beginning to regret the Egg McMuffin he'd chowed down on the way here. He dropped his head into his hands and massaged his temples. "What?" he said, without looking up.

"Listen, this is kind of serious."

Josh raised his head wearily. "What—" Josh broke off as a McMuffin burp escaped.

"Listen to me. There's a scam going on right under your nose. Someone is siphoning KiwiSaver contributions from the employees. It's only been going on for a couple of months, but they're taking quite a lot. The money goes to an international account, and I'm pretty sure I know whose it is. In about five minutes, I think I'm going to have proof."

Josh groaned.

PAIGE BLEW OUT a gust of air and continued pacing the kitchen. She didn't know what to do. When she'd arrived home last night, Tim had been going through a recipe book and when she'd asked what he was doing, he'd happily announced that they were having the neighbours over for dinner when they got back from their trip to Wellington. She'd stared at him, unsure about what to say. It felt like some sort of rebellion. But against what?

Then there were Sophie's messages telling her not to go into work and not to do anything until they spoke, but when Paige called her back she hadn't picked up.

All she could do right now was fester until either Sophie or Eddie got back to her.

She would go into S & S Investigations, she decided. She had to do something.

As she set about finishing the last half of her coffee, she opened Facebook. Straight away she saw Sophie had been tagged by Josh in a selfie taken at Vivace. Paige was surprised. Not that they were having a drink—she knew they'd gone there to celebrate after the presentation—but from this photo it appeared they'd gotten a bottle of wine and ordered food too. Sophie was smiling, but it was her uncertain smile. It was her—get me out of here—smile that Paige had seen many, many times. Paige was not good at reading facial expressions, but this one she knew. A snake of worry appeared in Paige's stomach. Had she left Sophie in an awkward situation? Paige was about to try Sophie again when she saw another notification.

This one really got her attention.

Leo had *liked Alice Garnet's photo*.

Her mother now had a Facebook account, and was *posting* things? And Leo was friends with her?

What bizarre world had she returned to?


SOPHIE DID NOT, as she'd been instructed by the fuming Josh, leave the building immediately. He'd been so enraged by her suggestion that someone in his department was fiddling the books that he'd risen from his desk glaring at her, fists clenched and knuckles whitening in a menacing manner, until she'd stumbled out of the room.

Sophie cast her eyes back toward Josh's office—the door was shut and the blinds were now closed—then went to collect Leo, who was waiting nervously in the corner by the water cooler.

"Did you get it?" Sophie said.

Leo nodded and Sophie high fived him.

"I couldn't print because I didn't know where the printer was, but I took screenshots and I emailed myself a copy." Leo held up his phone. "This should be enough. What do we do now? Where's that guy Josh?"

"He's not on board," Sophie said grimly. After thinking for a moment, she said, "Okay. Can you send me the evidence?" Leo nodded and busied himself with this phone. A moment later Sophie's phone pinged. "Thank you so much for your help, Leo, but you'd probably better go now."

"But—"

"I don't want to have to explain who you are to Denise. It won't help with what I have to do next."

"Okay," Leo grumbled.

Sophie first went to find the Source of All Knowledge—Sharon—but when she couldn't locate her, she went to find the Person that Made Things Happen—Denise. After a couple of minutes, she spotted her waiting at a printer down the corridor. Feeling very much like Paige, Sophie marched over to her and demanded Denise tell her the identity of the kind-eyed older man who had been in those executive meetings. Both times she'd been too nervous to remember details like names, but if needed, she could describe him well enough for a police sketch artist.

"You must mean Neil Fontenoy," Denise said after listening carefully to Sophie's breathless but perfect description.

"Great. Where is he?"

"You can't just turn up. You have to make an appointment with his assistant."

"Okay, where is she?"

"Level fourteen." Denise narrowed her eyes. "What's this about?" Denise had never liked Josh and she'd happened to see Sophie go into his office then come out again looking red-faced and flustered. "Did Josh do something?"

"Umm." Sophie eyed Denise, picking up on the hostility and wondering if this was the fastest route to seeing Neil. "Sort of." Sophie would explain everything properly to Neil, but it was imperative she got in front of him ASAP.

Denise set her lips into a tight line. "Come with me."

Sophie and Denise rode the elevator to the fourteenth floor in silence—Denise was not one for small talk—and located Neil's assistant halfway down the corridor.

"Hello Denise. You after Neil? He's about to join a conference call."

"It's important," Denise barked.

Neil's assistant's eyes widened, and even though she was higher up in the hierarchy than Denise, she nodded quickly and said, "You can have five minutes."

Denise's powers reached beyond the tenth floor, it seemed.

Ten minutes later, Denise and Sophie were back in the elevator, but this time with Neil Fontenoy in tow. Sophie had backed the right horse in picking Denise to help her with this task. Neil apparently took Denise as seriously as everyone else did. When they'd entered his office, Denise had told him Sophie had something important to say, he'd said, "Well if Denise thinks it's important, I'm ready to listen." Denise, a pleased blossom of colour spreading over her cheeks, had clucked to herself with pleasure.

The elevator dinged and the door opened. The three of them turned right and headed toward the two offices along the north wall.

"Hey!" Denise cried suddenly, startling both Sophie and Neil. "Stop!"

They both turned to see Michelle scurrying toward the stairs. "She never takes the stairs," Denise barked, her eyes ablaze. "She's making a run for it."

In those heels? Sophie thought, eyeing the three-inch stiletto ankle boots.

In a burst of motion Denise surged forward, breaking into an unexpectedly quick stride. As Sophie and Neil watched with wide-eyes, Denise leapt forward and tackled Michelle around the waist, bringing her crashing to the ground.

"Got you," Denise puffed.

THE VIBE IN the conference room was tense. Two security guards stood outside and the police had been called. Sophie sat next to Neil, with Denise and Josh on his other side and Michelle, whose mouth was set in a grim line, at the opposite end of the table. She crossed her arms and sniffed, looking out the window as if she didn't care what was going on, but Sophie thought Michelle was only hanging on to this calm façade by a thread.

"What the hell is going on?" Josh snapped. "Sorry, Neil," he added, "but this is ridiculous. She's feeding you nonsense." Josh waved his hand in Sophie's direction.

Sophie couldn't look at him because his anger was palpable.

"Josh, listen," Neil said.

"She's a disgruntled consultant. I had to let her go and now she's making up stories. Everything is fine in my department, Neil, I keep a close eye on things here, you know that." Josh's voice took on a cajoling tone.

"Is the payroll system offline and did you download the payroll reports from the last six months?" Neil asked.

Josh nodded sulkily and pushed a USB over to him.

"She has hard evidence, Josh, we can't ignore that. Harry King, one of your payroll clerks, has provided her with a copy of the report which clearly shows the discrepancy, and she also has a screenshot of the offshore bank account in Michelle's name, into which the missing money has been transferred. How she managed to get this information I do not know," Neil paused to flick his eyes to Sophie, "but the fact remains that there is evidence that Michelle here has been defrauding our company for a couple of months now."

"But how?" Josh said, his voice whiny. "What's she supposed to have done?"

"Instead of authorising payroll with the KiwiSaver contributions submitted by first Kate, then Harry, she changed the numbers and redirected the rest to her offshore account."

"What's she still doing here, then? Why would someone sit around and wait to get caught?"

Sophie cleared her throat. "It seems as if she was waiting for one last payroll to go through before she did a runner. She has flights booked to Spain in two days, I, uh, found her e-tickets." Sophie turned to Michelle to ask, "What happened to Kate? Chloe, Kate's neighbour, identified you. She said you'd been to visit Kate before she was found... dead."

Michelle sniffed again and stared resolutely at Sophie. "I'm not saying anything until I speak to a lawyer."

"Can I say something?" Denise asked.

"Of course," Neil replied.

"Kate's leave wasn't submitted in the normal way. When it came through it had already been authorised by Michelle. That almost never happens." Denise sat up straighter in her chair. "I don't think Kate submitted it at all. I think it was you," she said to Michelle.

"Was it an accident?" Sophie said softly. Michelle looked down as Sophie continued. "Kate discovered what you'd been up to and you went to Kate's house to confront her. Or maybe she asked to talk to you about it. And then, what... you got into a fight? There was a struggle? You pushed her and she fell and hit her head?"

Michelle's lower lip trembled.

"And then you came up with the idea to make it look as if she was packing to go on holiday and had fallen and hit her head, but you needed a paper trail to support this story, so you submitted leave on her behalf. Isn't that right?"

A tear slid down Michelle's cheek.

"Oh, Michelle," Neil said into the silence.

TEN MINUTES AFTER the police had taken Michelle away Josh was still fuming. He could not believe what was happening. He might lose his job over this. And it was all Sophie's fault. How dare she? First she rejects him and now this? He was livid. After she'd told him her insane theory and he'd told her to leave, she'd gone over his head and convinced that old softie Neil to listen to her. Sophie's audacity was mind-blowing. Who did she think she was, turning his life upside down like this?

Josh arrived on the third floor just in time to see Sophie exiting her meeting room.

"Sophie!" His eyes burned with anger. "I want a word with you."

# 16

When Paige arrived at S & S she found an ambulance double-parked outside the building.

She raced up the stairs two at a time. At the top, Hazel was being wheeled out of her office on a stretcher. Her eyes were closed, she was pale, and she had an oxygen mask strapped to her face.

"What happened?"

No one answered. She grabbed at one of the paramedics and yanked his arm until he turned to her with a frown.

"Who are you? Are you family?"

Paige hesitated, then said, "No."

"And all I can tell you is she collapsed. She found her," he gestured at a wide-eyed woman dressed in a courier outfit who was hovering near the door.

"Let's go," he said to colleague.

"Wait. I can call her nephew. Where are you going? Auckland City Hospital?"

The paramedic gave Paige a curt nod and they took her down the stairs.

Just then there was a loud and unmistakable thump from 2B. Paige immediately went over and banged on the door. "Hello?"

Empty offices don't make thumping noises.

Paige fished Hazel's keys out of her bag and found the one that fit into the 2B lock. Her hands shaking from adrenaline, Paige pushed the door. She paused on the threshold, waiting for sudden noise or motion, but there was none.

"Hello?" she said again. "I heard you, whoever you are. I know you're there."

This was not at all true. This office felt vacant. But she could feel a breeze. She went further inside and saw that in the office to the right, the window at the back was open. She raced over and peered out. There was no one to be seen, but there was a fire escape leading from the window to the ground. It was therefore possible for someone to access this office without a key. But why? Thumping around for the fun? Perhaps it was a homeless person or a squatter who was sleeping in here? Paige cast her eyes around the furniture-less space. But surely there would be evidence of that. Paige made a frustrated noise and was about to leave when she remembered the last time she was here there'd been a charger plugged into the wall. She went over to the corner and saw that it was gone. Someone had definitely been in here—was it just to charge their phone?

There was no time to ponder on this further. There was a woman on her way to the hospital that needed her help.

As Paige raced down the stairs she tried Eddie but he wasn't picking up so she left him a message and sent him a text just in case. She then tried Sophie, but she wasn't picking up either.

It took Paige over an hour to get to the hospital, locate a parking spot—she ended up having to park fifteen minutes away in the Domain—and find Hazel's hospital room. She slipped inside to see a nurse and a doctor standing over Hazel, one on each side of the bed. The nurse was taking vitals and the doctor was looking at her chart.

"Do we have any information about her GP?" the doctor said.

"I can look it up. Why?"

"I need to talk to them about the meds she's been prescribed. Her levels are all over the place." He shook his head. "This bloodwork doesn't look good at all."

"A-ha!" Paige cried.

The two health professionals turned and noticed Paige standing at the foot of the bed.

"Where did you come from?" The doctor said glaring at her. "And who are you?"

"She's not up for visitors," the nurse added.

"But... I'm her family."

The nurse narrowed her eyes and took a step toward Paige. "Even if you are, now is not the time." She shooed her out.

In the corridor, Paige stopped and took stock of what she'd heard. Hazel wasn't taking medication, she'd said so herself, and her GP in Dunedin had virtually confirmed it, without saying the actual words. So, if Hazel's blood tests revealed the presence of drugs in her system, how did they get there?

Paige pulled out her phone and called Sophie again but it continued to ring and ring. "*Pick up*, Sophie," she hissed.

The nurse emerged from Hazel's room. "She's stable," she said, "but you're not allowed in there, not right now." The nurse gave Paige a stern look. "You can come back for visiting hours."

Paige knew she wasn't going to get any further here, now that her cloak of invisibility had been yanked off, so she went back to the S & S offices. The door to Hazel's office was still open so she went straight inside. Paige needed more information, maybe even evidence, and since she'd already been through Hazel's office, the only other place she could think to look was Hazel's home. But she didn't know where Hazel lived. Paige rummaged through the drawers and the filing cabinet again, but it wasn't until she noticed a power bill sitting in Hazel's 'out' tray that she hit pay dirt. It wasn't a bill for the office, it was for a residence in Mt Eden. Paige grabbed the bill and scurried out to her car with Hazel's keys clutched in her hand.

TEN MINUTES LATER, Sophie let herself into S & S, still shaken by her encounter with Josh.

She made herself a cup of chamomile tea and sat at her computer, trying to relax. She took deep breaths, using her lower belly, and exhaled slowly, telling herself that everything was okay. She had solved the case, hadn't she? They now knew that the KiwiSaver contributions were being siphoned out and could take the appropriate steps to recover the money. People wouldn't be conned out of their retirement money. Or, maybe at least not as much as they could have been? Sophie took another sip of tea. Overall, she felt good about what she'd done, but she'd never seen anyone as angry as Josh had been and she was still rattled by that confrontation in the lift. Sophie was desperately trying to take a leaf out of Paige's book and shed the incident like a used skin, but it was difficult. Josh had had revenge in his eyes. Not to mention, as Sophie discovered upon opening her email account, he'd already sent her three emails, blaming her for everything.

When Sophie's phone beeped she sucked in a breath, wondering if Josh was now going to attack her via FB messenger, but it wasn't from him. It was from Hannah.

All the first message said was, *Hi.*

*Hi,* Sophie wrote back, biting the inside of her lip as she stared at the display.

*Did you get anything when Dad died?*

Sophie drew back, recoiling as if this had been a physical assault.

Was *that* what this was about? Hannah didn't want to connect with her new half-sister, she wanted money? Sophie had suspected her motives weren't particularly pure, but this seemed so callous. Sophie has always wanted a sister. And now it appeared she might have the classic evil half-sister instead of the kindred spirit she'd always imagined.

*Just curious*, Hannah added.

*No, I didn't*, Sophie replied.

Sophie watched as three dots appeared, then disappeared. This happened again. Then, instead of a message, a photo came through. It was a selfie of Hannah at a bar somewhere. Sophie shook her head. What was the point of that photo? She waited and waited, but nothing else came through. She noticed there was a missed call from Paige but she ignored this and put her phone down with a sigh, trying to push away the uneasy feeling in her stomach.

There was a thump from somewhere out in the hall. This was followed by a clattering sound. Was this the start of the renovations, Sophie wondered, but the noises had sounded as if they were coming from Hazel's place. When there was another thump from across the landing, Sophie thought perhaps she should check that these noises were not someone burgling the place. She left her phone on the desk and went to investigate.

She was correct, the noises had been coming from Hazel's office, and just inside the door stood the guy Sophie had seen with Simone in the supermarket. Clutched in his sweaty hand was a plastic bag filled with, Sophie couldn't tell what, but there were various lumps and a shiny packet of something.

"Um. Hi?" Sophie said.

"Oh. I'm Eddie. My aunt owns this place."

"Your aunt is Hazel?"

"Yeah?" Eddie eyed her. "Um... uh, who are you?"

Sophie stopped herself from reacting and forced her shoulders up and down into a shrug. He obviously didn't remember her from that time at Galbraith's when he and Simone came over to their table briefly. Or maybe he did but thought *she* wouldn't recall him. "Sophie. I work across there." She tried to keep her tone casual. "So, I haven't seen you around before." If he was going to pretend he hadn't seen her before, she would go along with it.

"I only moved up recently. After my mum, uh, died."

"Oh, I'm sorry."

"Hazel's my only family, now, so I thought I should be here with her. With everything going on."

Sophie nodded. "You came to Auckland at the same time as Hazel?"

Eddie swallowed then nodded. Footsteps sounded on the stairs behind Sophie. She turned around to see Simone.

Upon spotting Sophie, she frowned. "Oh, hello."

"Hi."

Simone looked past Sophie to Eddie. "Hello there. You're Hazel's nephew, aren't you?"

Sophie watched a few different emotions and expressions cross Eddie's face before he landed on a wide-eyed one. "Y-yes. Hello."

"Is Hazel around? I came by for a quick catch-up."

"Uh…"

Simone glared at Eddie, who was still wide-eyed.

"She's in hospital."

Now both Sophie and Simone stared at Eddie.

"She is?" Sophie said. "What happened?"

"She has dementia," Eddie said bluntly, looking past Sophie. "Hey, I better go."

"Yes, me too," Simone said, clip-clopping down the stairs.

Sophie watched them both leave with a kind of numb amazement. They were pretending they didn't know each other—and doing a terrible job of it—but why? And since when did Hazel have dementia?

Sophie returned to the S & S office deep in thought. Something was bugging her. Multiple things, in fact. If Eddie had only moved up when Hazel returned to Auckland a few weeks ago, then how had Sophie seen him before then hanging out at the pub with Simone. And why were they pretending they didn't know each other? It was a small thing that might be easily explained by the presence of other partners and adultery, but Sophie thought the whole thing reeked of something more.

Sophie picked up her phone. She now had two missed calls from Paige. Sophie stuck her tongue out at her phone—possibly the most childish thing she'd done in the last five years, but it was exactly how she felt. She shouldn't have had to deal with

Josh, and all that mess, on her own. Sophie doubted Josh even remembered Paige existed, so she would be shouldering all of Josh's rancour herself. And where was Paige, anyway? In Dunedin, for God knows what reason. She'd probably been whisked away for a mini-break by the doting Tim. He probably surprised her with some amazing trip, Sophie thought bitterly.

Sophie took a breath and tried to relax. She knew she couldn't blame Paige for the Josh situation, not really, but still, instead of calling Paige back, she texted Leo.

PAIGE PULLED UP outside Hazel's place. It was a small bungalow with a white gate and a tidy-looking garden at the front.

Paige let herself in the front door and called out, "Hello?" With no response, she immediately started snooping through the kitchen directly to her left. One half of the kitchen was pristine and the other messy, home to a box of cocoa-puffs, a carton of milk, several dirty-looking utensils, and a cereal bowl with a congealed substance in the bottom. Paige could not imagine Hazel eating cocoa-puffs. With a little more nosing and the discovery of male-sized running shoes and a coat in the hall, Paige realised Eddie must live here, or at least be staying with her. "Hello?" Paige called out again, just in case.

Paige cast her eye around the kitchen, then started opening cupboards. The doctor at the hospital had said there were drugs in her bloodstream, but Hazel said she didn't believe in medication. So maybe there was something here in her kitchen that could explain it? Maybe she was one of those people that took heaps of vitamins and herbal supplements and that was what had made her sick. Hazel did not seem like the kind of women to take alternative medicine either. Still, it was worth a look.

In the pantry—again, organized into one tidy side and one messy side—Paige found the packet of protein powder she'd seen Hazel use to make her lunchtime smoothies. Her eyes moved past this, then returned. The packet was unopened, but there was something weird about the seal—it looked unnaturally bumpy or something. On closer inspection Paige could not find anything wrong, so she replaced it and closed the pantry door.

It was a small house but it held three bedrooms. One bedroom was clearly Hazel's, the other occupied by her messy houseguest, and the remaining one set up as a home office. Paige was about to look in Hazel's room—perhaps there was something on her nightstand or in a bedside table drawer? —when she heard the unmistakeable sound of keys at the front door. She lurched into the door to her right. It was the bathroom. As Paige waited breathlessly by the door, she asked herself what she was doing. It was probably just Eddie returning home. So why was she hiding? Coming up with an explanation for this would be difficult. In the absence of a clear course of action, Paige stayed where she was.

Heavy footsteps entered the house, there was a metallic clang as keys were thrown onto the hall table, then the footsteps trudged into the kitchen. Paige leaned against the bathroom door wondering whether she could find a way to slip out and then knock on the front door and ask after Hazel— which would've been the normal way to go about things. As Paige pondered the problem, her eyes drifted over to the medicine cabinet above the sink.

Since she was in here, she might as well look.

From beyond the door, Paige heard Eddie turn on the tap in the kitchen, then gulp noisily. Was he drinking directly from the faucet? Paige wondered briefly, before leaning forward to open the cabinet door.

Eddie let out a loud burp.

Inside the cabinet, there were four small bottles of medication. Hazel *does* believe in medicine, Paige thought at first, but then she saw they were not prescribed for Hazel, but for an Edward Stevens. There was a bottle of Benadryl and three prescriptions. One was for Doxycycline, which Paige knew to be a generic all-purpose antibiotic, and it was out of date, but the other two were current prescriptions. Something called Elavil, and another called Anafril.

"That's right," Paige whispered to herself. Hazel had mentioned Eddie had allergies and took meds for depression. Paige pressed her ear against the door and heard clattering in the kitchen, so she returned to the cabinet. She eyed the medication again, then pulled out her phone and opened a search engine. She typed in the drug names and scrolled through the results, then opened another tab to further investigate.

As she made sense of the results of her search, her chest grew tight with excitement. She was starting to get an inkling of what was going on. Paige was about to call Sophie again until she realised that Eddie might hear her, so instead she sent her a text message.

*Get Roman on standby. I think I know what's happening with Hazel. Will text again with details.*

Paige took a few photos, making sure she got all the medicine bottles in shot, and was about to try to sneak out when she heard heavy footsteps coming down the hall. She looked around frantically. There was only a tiny window above the toilet. She was small, but was she small enough? Paige stepped closer to inspect its size. Eddie sneezed, just outside the door, a loud and trumpeting sound. Paige startled and dropped her phone into the toilet bowel.

"Dammit," she cried without thinking.

The door knob rattled. "Who's in there?" Eddie demanded. Paige held her breath. "Who is it? Open the door," he cried, now banging his fists against the door.

Paige backed up until she was against the wall. How the hell was she going to get out of this?

SOPHIE'S PHONE BUZZED again. This time it was a text. When she read the message she sat bolt upright. "Oh, no."

When Leo ambled into the S & S office a few moments later, Sophie was staring at her phone with wide eyes.

"What's wrong?"

Sophie's attempts to call Paige were going straight to voice mail.

"It's Paige. I'm worried."

"About?"

"Paige left this cryptic message about Hazel, the lady who owns this building, and now her phone is off. But she said to get Roman on standby."

"What do you think's going on?"

Sophie shrugged helplessly.

"Maybe you should call Roman."

"And say what? Paige wants you on standby?"

"You got a weird message from Paige and you're worried about her."

Sophie nodded. "Can I text?"

Leo shrugged and said, "Sure."

But Sophie knew what the correct answer was and reluctantly dialled Roman's number. When he didn't pick up, she didn't know if she was relieved or not. She didn't have to have an awkward conversation with him, but what if Paige needed police assistance urgently?

"No answer. I'll text." Sophie typed out a quick message, hoping it made sense.

"What do we do in the meantime?" Leo asked.

"I don't know." Sophie said. "Let's try and figure out what's going on."

"How?"

"We work the clues." Sophie started pacing the space between her and Paige's desks. Leo copied her, following her as she moved from one end of the office to the other. "Apparently, or at least accordingly to Eddie, Hazel suddenly has dementia."

"What do you mean suddenly?"

"Exactly."

Leo nodded even though he had no idea what Sophie was on about.

"And then there's Eddie, Hazel's nephew, and Simone, Hazel's property manager, hanging around the building, pretending they don't know each other. They were acting super suspiciously. So, what's this all about?" Sophie paused to look out the window. The window was shut but air was still escaping through a crack at the bottom which seemed to be getting bigger. They'd decided to let it go since renovations were already planned.

Renovations.

"Hang on," Sophie said, turning to Leo. "What's the central thing, the common denominator?"

Leo looked confused. Understandably so, since he'd only been exposed to the briefest, most superficial pieces of this particular puzzle. "Hazel?"

"Yes. But also, this building. Right? That's what connects Simone to Hazel."

"Okay..." Leo eyed Sophie, wondering where she was going with this.

"Something's going on here, Leo. We've got to find Paige. Can you trace her phone?"

"Not if it's switched off."

"Um. Okay. Let me think."

Paige, being Paige, would be embroiled right in the middle of this. The question was where?

"What about Hazel Berryman. Can you find out where she lives?"

SOPHIE SAT IN her car. She was parked right behind Paige's car, which was outside Hazel's house. Sophie hadn't gone inside yet because Roman was on his way. He'd called her back and she'd told him, breathlessly and awkwardly, the situation as she knew it. Sophie had then texted

Leo, who'd gone to check Paige's house, to let him know.

Now, after five minutes of waiting, Sophie couldn't stand it any longer and got out of the car. Who knew when Roman was going to get here? What if he had some other police emergency to deal with? Sophie had to get inside, and now. That Paige's phone had been suddenly switched off seemed altogether ominous. Sophie's chest felt tight as she surveyed the outside of the house. She could knock on the front door and ask if everything was okay, but what if this made them freak out and do something to Paige? No, she needed to sneak in and find out what was going on, without anyone knowing about it. Roman had said he wasn't far away, so she had to hope this was true.

There was a largish window on each side of the house and the one on the left was less visible from the road, so that was the one she'd try to climb through.

ROMAN ARRIVED AT the address Sophie had given him but there was no sign of her anywhere.

Before knocking on the door, he did one circuit of the house. Coming around the back he discovered someone hanging half out of the window.

"Sophie? Is that you?"

He was trying not to look too closely at her bottom, but it was difficult because with her half-in-and-half-out position, it was being rather nicely framed by the window.

"Go inside," Sophie puffed as she craned her head toward Roman. "You have to rescue Paige."

"From what I can see, the only person I should be rescuing is you."

"No. You have to kick in the door. Or something."

Sophie swung her legs at the approaching Roman.

"Oomph. Ow. Dammit, Sophie."

"Sorry."

"Stop struggling. Just—"

"Go get Paige then come help me."

"Fine."

ONCE ROMAN HAD gone, Sophie, motivated by the unpleasant possibility of Roman having to push her buttocks through the window or drag her through from the other side, found the strength for one more kick and this was the one that enabled her to wriggle the rest of her body inside.

She was in a bedroom. It was empty, thank goodness. As she crept to the door, she could admit to herself at least one of those kicks at Roman had been on purpose and related to the existence of Anya.

When she got to the hall she found Roman and Paige standing there, looking a little too relaxed and casual, given the panic with which she'd raced over here and broken into Hazel's house.

"What's going on?" Sophie asked.

"Her nephew Eddie was here, but he took off. I was in the bathroom and he heard me and was trying to get inside, but then he got a phone call and stopped banging on the door and went to his room, rummaged around for a bit, and then left. When I was sure he'd gone, I came out of the bathroom, and found Roman."

Roman got out his phone. "He probably knows you're onto him and is doing a runner." Paige had already given Roman a very brief rundown of the situation with Hazel and Eddie. "Last chance to tell me if this is something I shouldn't be wasting police resources on?"

Paige nodded. "Do it."

"Okay, I'll see if I can get eyes on his car. What's his full name?"

"Edward, uh..." Paige checked the bottle of pills, she'd taken from Hazel's cabinet, now clutched in her hand. "Edward Stevens." She handed them over to Sophie. "Check them out," she said.

While Roman made the call, Paige and Sophie huddled together in the hall and said at exactly the same time, "I think I know what's going on."

# 17

Hazel's hospital room was empty.

Paige, Sophie, and Roman looked at each other, wondering if this was as ominous as it seemed, but as they exited the room to look for her in the nearby areas Hazel appeared at the end of the corridor, being wheeled toward them by a nurse.

Paige charged toward them. "Hazel, are you okay?"

Hazel was pale and weak-looking, but she managed a small smile. "I've been better, but I'm not done yet."

The nurse wheeled Hazel into her room but held up her hand when Paige tried to follow. "The doctor is coming to check a few things, after that, you can visit."

"But we're not visiting, he's a police officer and—"

"After. That. You. Can. Visit."

Paige took a seat on one of the chairs outside the room.

"I'll let Leo know what's going on," said Sophie, typing out a text. When she looked up and noticed Roman was only a few feet away, she started walking backward in the opposite direction. "Um. Going to find the toilet."

Roman's shoulders slumped as he watched her go. With a sigh he took out his phone and made a call, ambling down the hall in the other direction as he talked.

With nothing to do but wait, Paige got her own phone out. Her mother had been on Facebook again and Paige was wondering if she was having some sort of midlife crisis. She went to her mother's timeline and saw, at the top of a series of inane updates—Alice Garnet had gotten the point of social media very quickly—was another photo Leo had liked. A selfie, with her mother wearing a coy smile and a shirt with *two buttons* undone at the top. But it was the caption that Paige was staring at.

*For my Lion.*

It only took Paige a second to join the dots.

Lion. As in Leo the Lion.

You have *got* to be kidding, Paige thought.

AS SOON AS the doctor emerged from Hazel's room, Paige stood up and lurched inside.

At the same time as Sophie returned from the toilets, a uniformed police officer appeared in the corridor with a miserable looking Eddie and a furious looking Simone.

"Thanks," Roman said to the officer, then gestured for Eddie and Simone to enter Hazel's room. He went after them and Sophie, hanging back a bit, entered last.

Inside, Hazel was reclining in bed, propped up by pillows. Paige stood next to the bed.

"I think it's time for a bit of chat, isn't it?" Roman said, nodding at Eddie and Simone.

"If you're feeling up to it, Hazel?" Sophie added.

Hazel coughed but nodded. "I'm rather interested to hear what all this is about."

The room fell quiet and everyone looked at Paige.

"Right, okay. So I—"

"Take it from the beginning though, okay, Paige? I need all the details," Roman said, pulling out his notepad.

"When I met Hazel, I was surprised by how on-to-it she was," Paige began. "How unlike an old lady she seemed."

"Thank you," Hazel said drily.

"But then the next couple of times I saw her she was disoriented and confused. And she nearly fainted."

"But dementia is a fluctuating illness. With periods of lucidity, then periods of confusion," Eddie said, sounding as if he was reciting something.

"Shut up," Simone said quickly, glancing at Roman.

"Yes, there are fluctuations, but not like that usually, and one doesn't normally deteriorate quite that quickly," Paige said. "And there's a better explanation," she said, raising her eyebrows and drawing out the moment. "Medicine cures problems, sure, but it almost always has side effects. For example, some medications have anticholinergic properties—which means the medication blocks the effect of acetylcholine on your brain."

"Acetylcholine is a neurotransmitter," Sophie added, addressing Hazel. "It's involved in messages between the brain and muscles. But it's also important for things like memory and attention."

"Blocking this neurotransmitter," Paige continued, "can create certain side effects. Symptoms like confusion, disorientation, poor coordination, dizziness, nausea, fatigue, even delirium. Symptoms which could mimic those of a neurodegenerative illness... such as dementia." Paige finished triumphantly.

"So what?" Simone said, folding her arms across her chest defiantly.

Paige held up one of the pill bottles. "Eddie is taking Benadryl, which is an anti-histamine that contains diphenhydramine, which has anti-cholinergic properties and is not recommended for people over sixty." Paige handed the bottle to Roman and held up the other two. "And he's also been prescribed Elavil, which contains amitriptyline, and Anafril which contains clomipramine. These have been used to treat things like depression and pain. But guess what kind of drug they use."

"An anti-cholin... Whatever that drug you said before was," Roman said.

"Exactly." She gave the bottles to Roman. "Eddie has drugs that have properties that could cause symptoms that mimic an illness like dementia. Especially if given to an old person."

Hazel narrowed her eyes at Eddie.

"So?" Eddie said, his voice sounding strained. "I've got those meds for proper things. Depression affects a lot of people, you know. And allergies. They're like... the most common illnesses, right?" He addressed this to Simone.

"Will you *shut up*," Simone hissed at Eddie with a ferocious glare.

"Carry on, Paige," Roman said, "I know where you're headed, but let's hear it."

"So those are prescribed for Eddie but when you compare their side effects to Hazel's symptoms... And if we ask the doctors to confirm what drugs Hazel has in her bloodstream, I'm sure we'll find a match, and since she hasn't been prescribed them herself, it's obvious. Eddie has been poisoning Hazel with his medications," Paige declared triumphantly.

Hazel shook her head sadly.

"And I've been thinking about how," Paige continued. "The seal on the protein packet in Hazel's pantry looks as if it might have been tampered with and when I think back to all the times Hazel fainted, or seemed weird, it was always after lunch. She told me she has one of her smoothies every day for lunch and Eddie, having lived with her, would have known that. It's the obvious choice. Eddie has been spiking her smoothies with his drugs."

"But why?" Roman asked.

"I have a theory," Sophie said, stepping forward. "It was all about the building, wasn't it? Hazel owns it and Eddie was trying to get Hazel considered not fit to make her own decisions, right?" Sophie paused to eye Eddie. "That way you could become a living executor of her estate and take control of her property."

"Yes!" Paige exclaimed. "Because even though Eddie was her only family, he wouldn't inherit it. I saw Hazel's will. Everything goes to charity!"

"How on earth have you seen my will?" Hazel said, then shook her head. "You know what? Never mind. I'm glad you did."

"It wasn't fair," Eddie suddenly whined. "The money should have been mine and Mum's anyway! She was going to leave it all to some stupid children's charity, which is probably a scam anyway, right Simone?"

Simone responded by elbowing him violently, but it didn't do any good because Eddie was now huffing and puffing, gathering up steam.

"Mum told me all about it. Mum and Dad went in with Hazel and Uncle John to buy the property, but then Hazel pulled a fast one, and convinced them to pull out of the venture and so they lost out—"

"Actually, you greedy little shit," Hazel interrupted. "It was the other way around." Hazel turned to address Sophie, Paige, and Roman. "When our parents died my sister and I received an inheritance. We agreed, Pearl and I, along with our husbands, to all go in together and buy into a new development on the waterfront. Pearl and Roger agreed to pay their half but it was myself and John who signed the papers, for some complicated legal reason, and then at the last minute Pearl and Roger pulled out. John and I tried to convince them to remain in the investment. We needed them, financially, but Roger convinced Pearl, the indulgent little shit that he was, to go on a world trip instead. So, they left us in the lurch and we risked everything to keep up with the payments. Finally, years and years later, after many *many* hard years of not having enough money and a massive debt, we got to a place where we were comfortable, and then the waterfront investment paid off."

Gosh, Sophie thought. For a nearly 80-year-old woman, Hazel said *shit* a lot.

"When the money ran out, Roger left Pearl. And when Pearl herself began to struggle with money, she re-wrote history, convincing herself that somehow John and I had conned her out of the property, which of course had gone on to become very valuable." Hazel swallowed. "John and I sold up and bought the Symonds Street property because I wanted a heritage building that I could work in, as well as a nest-egg so John could retire and we could be comfortable." Hazel looked down for a moment. "Pearl, rest in peace, was always a champion grudge holder. She must have told Eddie her version of history, so he thought he was entitled, but..." She broke off to eye Eddie first, then let her gaze rest on Simone. "I can't imagine he thought up this whole scheme himself. I imagine someone in property probably had something to do with exactly how Eddie planned to get what he thought he was owed."

Simone and Eddie were quiet.

"Actually, I'd already noticed Simone sniffing around a little too eagerly," Hazel said. "I'd even considered hiring you girls to look into it. Your presence here, Eddie, to look after me? It did not seem altogether genuine. I've a nose for these things," Hazel added, nodding to herself.

Paige silently groaned. They'd been so close to being hired, and paid, for this case.

"My sister's voice. That was you, wasn't it?" Hazel said quietly to Eddie. "I heard it floating through the office, faintly but surely. I thought I was losing my mind. But that was you."

"From 2B!" Paige cried. "You played a recording from your phone. That's why there was a charger in there."

"To make me think I was hearing things, and to hopefully convince other people I was delusional," Hazel said.

Eddie looked down.

Hazel made a sad clucking noise. "I imagine it was Simone who knew, being in real estate, that my only living relative was the most likely person to get power of attorney, and this would give you control over the property," Hazel continued.

"And hardly a week goes by without some mention in the paper of the growing scourge of dementia," Sophie said.

"With a bit of research, they worked out which drugs would work." Paige said, turning to Roman. "If you check both of their laptops you'll probably find it all in their search histories."

Simone and Eddie were looking rather grey.

"And once you'd figured out which medications you needed to cause symptoms of dementia, you went to some relaxed doctor to get a prescription, right?" Paige said.

"There's no blood test you can do for depression, and nowadays it's so common that a lot of doctors wouldn't think too hard about prescribing for it," Sophie added.

"So, you crushed up the meds and put them in her protein powder, but you screwed up the dose, or mixed up the medications or something, and you nearly killed her."

"We never meant to kill you," Eddie said to Hazel, his voice anguished. "Just—"

"Get me diagnosed with dementia and committed to an institution so you could take all my assets?" Hazel said, delivering her famous one eyebrow arch.

# 18

Roman gave Paige and Sophie a lift back to their cars, both of which were still at Hazel's place. He pulled up outside and turned off the engine. "Here you go. Listen..." His head was angled more than halfway toward Sophie who was in the back seat, but he didn't finish his thought and the moment hung with the three of them sitting awkwardly in the silence.

Finally, Paige said. "I've got to go see Mum. Thanks for coming to help us, Roman. I appreciate it. I'll see you later."

"No worries," Roman said, his gaze fixed on Sophie.

"Um. Okay," Sophie said, quickly unbuckling so she could get out of the car at the same time as Paige. They walked across the road together while Roman stayed in the car.

"See you back at the office?" Paige said at her car. "About an hour?"

"Sure." Sophie went over to the Jetta, all too aware that Roman had not yet driven off.

Roman, sitting like a statue in the driver's seat, suddenly lurched out of his car and across the road. He reached Sophie as she was opening the car door. He pushed it shut.

"I'm sorry, Sophie. Okay? I'm sorry..."

But he couldn't finish, because by apologising for having a wife, Roman would be admitting something. And even though it was true, would it help anything?

Sophie faced him, only the quiver of her chin betraying the emotions she was struggling to control. Finally, tortured by the silence, she said, "How could you?"

Roman brought one hand up to run it through his short hair before saying sadly, "I didn't..."

A painful contraction in Sophie's stomach reminded her that he hadn't, not really. He hadn't done anything. It was her stupid imagination. She'd gotten carried away all on her own.

And so they stood there, facing each other, while the million things they wanted to say were left unsaid.

PAIGE STOOD IN front of her mother, feet planted and arms crossed.

"I'm not wrong, am I? What I saw on Instagram? You and Leo?"

Alice conceded a nod.

"How did this happen?"

"We spent quite a lot of time together over the past couple of weeks. In the garden. We chatted and got to know each other and he's really a rather lovely young man.

"How far has it gone?" Paige's eyes widened. "You haven't...?"

"It's none of your business."

"How could you?"

"What do you mean? I have every right to a romantic life."

"Gross, Mum."

"Excuse me?"

"Did it have to be with my colleague? And he's young enough to be your son."

"You sent him to me, after all."

"This isn't what I had in mind. Are you, like, together? Is this something serious?" Images of Leo attending family Christmas as her mother's date and them canoodling and wearing matching outfits (for some reason) popped into Paige's mind. "Mum? Is this serious?"

Alice lifted her shoulders and looked off into the distance, a smile creeping onto her face. "Perhaps. But for now, as you young people call it, we're *hanging out*."

God, this was mortifying, thought Paige. Why was this happening to her? Paige took small angry steps from one end of the kitchen to the other and back again, but abruptly stopped, deflated. "But..." She cast forlorn eyes to her mother. "What about Dad?"

SOPHIE WAS BACK at the S & S offices, reliving that last conversation with Roman, her arms wrapped around herself, wondering if she should have said something different. Her whole body ached with misery. How could she want someone she'd only known for a short time, so badly? She brushed away a tear and yanked a tissue from the supply in her drawer. After blowing her nose she pushed her shoulders back and took a shaky breath.

"Hey," Paige said, banging open the door.

Sophie looked up to see that Paige's eyes were moist and her expression glum.

"What's wrong?"

Paige opened her mouth, then closed it, then sighed. "You know what? I'm not ready to talk about it yet."

"Is it about your mum?"

Paige nodded, pushed her lower lip out a little further, and looked down.

Sophie got up, went over to her friend, and pulled her into a hug.

After a moment, she leaned back and studied Paige's face. Sophie wanted to tell her about Roman and about Hannah; and it was clear that Paige had something to share with her too, but it wasn't the right time. Right now, they needed to remind themselves of why they were doing this in the first place. Right now, they needed to celebrate their successes.

"Guess what. I uncovered a KiwiSaver scam."

"What?" Paige clutched at Sophie's hands. "OMG, you have to tell me everything."

They clattered into the second room and Paige took the bottle of Pinot Noir she'd taken from her mother's and the bag of Kettle Fry chips she'd picked up from the dairy down the road and placed them on the table.

Sophie widened her eyes to show her appreciation. "Good thinking."

And so, they each told the other about the events leading to the discovery of not one but two devious schemes.

PAIGE TOOK ANOTHER handful of chips. "So that Michelle woman's been carted off by the police?"

Sophie nodded. "She was talking lawyers but I think she'll end up admitting what she did."

"Do you think it was an accident? Kate's death."

Sophie tilted her head. "Yeah. I mean, I don't think Michelle went there to kill her, but... you never know."

"Since you uncovered that scam, do you think they'll want us to do more work?"

"Honestly? They weren't exactly thrilled about it."

"But we still get paid?"

"For the work we've done yes, but I suspect they're going to be too embarrassed to keep us on there. And they've already sent an email to remind us about the non-disclosure agreements we signed."

"What about Josh?"

Sophie shook her head. "It got really nasty, Paige. He was so angry when I turned him down. And he's going to take some of the blame because payroll is within his department and he should have been keeping an eye on that stuff."

"But he can't blame you for him not doing his job."

Sophie shrugged. "Can't he?" She looked down. "But the good news is I think with the non-disclosure he won't be able to say anything bad about us either. So at least there's that..." Sophie trailed off and tears threatened behind her eyes.

"What's up?"

"I felt a bit abandoned. I know you had a good reason not to show up to drinks with Josh, but... I mean," Sophie looked up at the ceiling, trying to gather her thoughts. "It's not even that, really. You know what I realised? We both went off to other *cities* without telling each other where we were going. I went to Hamilton and you went to Dunedin." Paige nodded sombrely as Sophie continued. "I mean, that's just dumb. Either of us could have ended up in trouble."

"Yeah, I'm not going to lie, that thing with Eddie was kind of freaky. I know he seems like a bit of a goober, but he did poison his aunt, so who knows what he is capable of. When he was banging on the bathroom door trying to get in..." Paige shook her head. "You were smart enough to take Leo with you, but yeah, let's not do that again."

"We're a great team, and one of the reasons for that is that our skills and personalities complement each other, but you're not half of a team when you're on your own."

"Agreed." Paige lifted her glass and Sophie clinked hers against it. "From now on, no avoiding, even if we're annoyed at each other."

"Definitely."

Paige sat up straighter. "Ooh. Let's make a code word, you know, in case one of us has to secretly communicate to the other that things are not okay."

"Yes." Sophie sat up too. "There should be a question and an answer. Like the person who's worried asks...." Sophie snapped her fingers. "I know. We could ask *hey did you feed the cat?*"

"And if something is wrong, the answer is *No, I forgot.*"

They grinned at each other and clinked glasses again.

"So, it seems like Hazel is going to be okay," Sophie said.

"Yeah, the drugs were already clearing from her system."

"What will happen to Eddie and Simone do you think?"

Paige shrugged. "Dunno. It all depends on how much actual evidence they can find that it was Eddie who put those drugs in her smoothies. I think he got a chance to get rid of a lot of evidence. But either way, I'm glad we stopped them."

Sophie stood up. "Hey, shall we do our ritual?"

"Yes!"

Paige retrieved two heavy tumblers from the cupboard and handed them to Sophie, then pulled out the bottle of whiskey. They both moved back into the main office and sat in the chairs under the window so the neon from the sign across the road flickered into the office and across their faces. Sophie set out the glasses and Paige uncapped the bottle of whiskey and poured a dash of the amber liquid into each of the tumblers. When they'd solved the case of The Disappearance of Polly

Dixon, Paige had brought out this bottle so they could celebrate like they did in the movies. Even though they'd quickly realised neither of them could stand the taste of whiskey, they both like the symbolism of the ritual.

"Here's to us," Paige said. "To solving two more cases."

"Except Hazel never hired us and we didn't get paid for solving—"

"Sssh," Paige said, raising her glass. "To S & S Investigations."

"To Squirrel and Swan," Sophie added.

### The End

# S & S Investigations: Solved Cases

1. The Remuera Pet Napper

2. The Disappearance of Polly Dixon

3. The Corporate Gig

4. The Mysterious Behaviour of Hazel Berryman

# Acknowledgements

Thank you to everyone who contributed to this book. Big thanks to my readers Julie, Lisa, Jane, and Becks; and special thanks to Mum for your love of grammar and for laughing out loud.

# Other Titles

### The Lucan Trilogy

A YA/NA Urban Fantasy series. Action and suspense with a kickass heroine and a supernatural twist. #1 Lucan; #2 Rogue; #3 Ultimatum

### The Unravel

Soul Harper has something to hide and Detective Nico Davis has something to prove. The unravel is inevitable.

### The Gemma Cross Series

Gemma Cross was going legit. She's trying to stay out of trouble, but will trouble keep finding her? #1 Gemma Cross Day One